Despite his casual tone, Della could see a glinting intensity in Luke's eyes. A trembling sensation filled the pit of her stomach. "I just... I thought you might..."

"Thought I might?" He moved closer. "Do this?" He touched his lips to the sensitive skin below her ear.

"Don't," she said, annoyed at how weak she sounded. Not the firm rebuttal she'd intended it to be.

"Why not?"

"Because...because friends don't do this."

"Do they do this?" He slid one hand around the nape of her neck and pulled her closer. She should stop him. She had to stop him. She couldn't let him kiss her.

His lips were as warm and firm as she'd always imagined. His kiss was tender, gentle, slow, making her own lips quiver. His strong arms slid around her waist and up her back, pulling her against him, drawing her closer still while he caressed her mouth.

Her insides melted.

Dear Reader,

If you've ever witnessed a couple take the journey from friends to lovers, you'll know that they didn't make the transition easily. It's rarely as simple as revealing an attraction. On the contrary, making the first move can be an agonizing decision.

Because the stakes are so much higher.

And there are plenty of potholes to stumble into on the way. There's a danger in taking a friendship where it's never gone before—not merely fear of rejection, but irreparable damage to the relationship they cherish. That's why it's so hard for them to take the ultimate risk.

To someone on the outside it can appear blindingly obvious that the two are meant to be together. She's his rock, his steadying influence. He's her pal, her confidant. They communicate well, enjoy each other's company. They're soul mates. So why can't they see it?

Because they're best friends. Instead, they hide their feelings, repress their lustful thoughts and channel their love into platonic caring and sharing. Until....

Whatever the catalyst, when friends do finally admit that there's more than friendship between them the result can be a deep, abiding love based on mutual respect, understanding and acceptance.

A love that's worth the risk.

Best wishes,

Claire Baxter

CLAIRE BAXTER
Best Friend...Future Wife

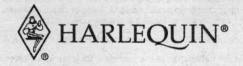

TORONTO • NEW YORK • LONDON
AMSTERDAM • PARIS • SYDNEY • HAMBURG
STOCKHOLM • ATHENS • TOKYO • MILAN • MADRID
PRAGUE • WARSAW • BUDAPEST • AUCKLAND

ISBN-13: 978-0-373-03966-1
ISBN-10:   0-373-03966-2

BEST FRIEND...FUTURE WIFE

First North American Publication 2007.

www.eHarlequin.com

Printed in U.S.A.

Claire Baxter talks to us about her new book

BEST FRIEND...FUTURE WIFE

"Foreign correspondents who travel to the world's most dangerous places see more than most people would see in ten lifetimes. When their courage is combined with values and a genuine desire to disclose what the world needs to know—not to entertain, but to find words to make sense of things—when they have the ability to engage people of all walks of life and treat them with respect, these people are true heroes.

But it's a lifestyle that takes a toll—one that can have far-reaching effects on a person's life. It takes a special kind of love to heal the heart of someone who's lived this life. I wanted Luke to find this special love with Della, and I hope you'll agree that he deserves it—that they deserve to find it together."

For Raelene—for the constant encouragement
and unconditional friendship

CHAPTER ONE

'PLEASE don't let it be Tom,' Della Davis muttered when her mobile phone rang.

She reached into her handbag with one hand and skilfully steered the car around the corner with the other. She didn't need another call from Tom Dermont, client from hell. She'd spent most of the day dealing with him, and he'd turned her mind to mush.

After coming to a standstill in the side street, she delved deeper into the large leather bag. Retrieving the phone from the very bottom, she steeled herself to see the caller's ID. If it was Tom again, she'd scream. Better yet, she'd resign.

The phone stopped ringing as she flipped it open. Great. She closed it with a snap and dropped it into her lap, sorely tempted to switch it off. But her conscience wouldn't let her. Nor would she resign. She had too much to lose, including the promotion she'd worked so hard for.

Still, she'd had enough of Tom for one day—her least favourite person at the best of times and, in a PR crisis like today's, her worst nightmare.

'Remind me why I love my job,' she said out loud.

Silence was the only response, and she shrugged, wincing at the stiffness in her shoulders. She needed a relaxing soak in her favourite lavender-scented bath foam.

Rolling her shoulders slowly, she pictured herself collapsing into bed...but not to sleep. Not to do anything normal people did in bed. Fat chance. She'd brought piles of work home, and she'd be sitting up with it till she fell asleep on the laptop. Again.

A beep from the phone made Della jump. Accessing her voicemail, she sighed with relief at the sound of her best friend's bright tones. She rang Lyn straight back. Just what she needed. The perfect antidote for the way she felt.

Lyn answered on the first ring. 'I'm in the car,' she said.

Della heard the familiar background track of Jamie, aged four, singing at the top of his voice and Cassie, six months, drowning him out with her wails.

'I have big news,' Lyn said.

Della rolled her eyes, but smiled at Lyn's excitement. 'Where are we going this time?'

'Where are we going?'

'I have more than enough shoes, Lynnie, so I hope it's not another—'

'No, no. It's not a sale. Not this time. Luke's coming home. For good.'

It took a moment for Lyn's words to register. Della blinked at the phone. '*What* did you say?'

'Shock, isn't it? Good one, though. I can't wait to see him.'

Too stunned to speak, Della wondered what she'd done to deserve this. On top of everything else. Today of all days.

'Shock' was an understatement. Oh, she'd known Luke would come home one day. He'd always said he wouldn't stay overseas for ever. But she'd expected to have some notice. Time to prepare herself before seeing him again. With his wife.

'Dell, hon? Are you there?'

Della snapped out of her trance. After years of hiding her feelings from Lyn, the last thing she needed was to give herself away now.

'Coming home?' Her voice sounded almost normal. 'You mean he and Yvonne are going to live here?'

'Had enough of living in India, apparently. Moving back to little old Adelaide and his loving family.' Lyn laughed. 'Incredible, isn't it?'

'It's—' Her tongue stuck to the roof of her mouth. She tried again. 'When?'

'You know my brother,' Lyn said. 'Loves his surprises, doesn't he? He rang from Melbourne while waiting for a connecting flight. So, Mum wants you there for dinner tonight.'

'Tonight…' Della's brain had gone into overload. It simply couldn't cope. She didn't know what to say.

'I'm on my way to Mum's now. Seven-thirty sharp. Okay?'

'But…' Della glanced at the digital display on the dashboard. 'I won't have time to get home and back again.'

'So don't. Come straight over. I've got some margarita mix and tequila on the seat next to me. I'll have a drink mixed and ready for you. I know how stressed you are after a day at work.'

'Not every day,' she murmured, while toying with the idea of declining. She couldn't. Lyn's mum had been more of a mother than her own ever had. She'd never disobeyed a summons from Dawn yet, and she wouldn't start now.

But. Luke. Would. Be. There.

'Oh, cripes. I forgot,' Lyn said. 'Here I am rabbiting on and…' Her tone changed, became softer. 'You had your appointment today, didn't you?'

The sympathy she heard in Lyn's voice made Della's breath catch in her chest.

'Yes,' she squeezed out.

And there'd been no time afterwards to lick her wounds. Her workload hadn't allowed for such self-indulgence.

'Dell, hon, what did the doctor say?'

The knowledge was too new. Too raw. 'Not yet,' she said. 'I'll tell you later.'

Jamie's voice filled Della's ear for a moment, then Lyn said, 'I'll make it a large margarita.'

Della clicked off the phone and dropped it into her bag. She needed that drink. Tom Dermont. Dr Morgan. Now Luke and Yvonne. What a day.

She had to pull herself together. It was lucky she was wearing one of her best business suits and had some make-up in her bag. She'd be presentable, at least. And it wasn't as though Luke had any inkling how she felt about him. She'd never made a fool of herself in front of him before and she wouldn't today.

She reached for the ignition, then hesitated, biting her lip. She couldn't do this. A fluttering sensation rose from her chest to her throat.

No. She wouldn't give in to anxiety.

She *could* do this. She was a crisis expert—the one her firm counted on to bring composure to chaos. She simply had to put on her work face, her mask.

Just like she had when he'd been over on his occasional visits during the last decade or so.

Just like she had when he'd brought his new bride home to meet the family a few years ago. She'd smiled and congratulated him as if she really had felt nothing more than a sisterly affection for him.

She'd fooled them then, she could do it again.

If only she'd had more time to get used to the idea of seeing the two of them together, living here.

Turning the car, she headed east. Lyn's parents lived in the same impressive house in the same leafy street in the same prestigious suburb where Lyn and Luke had grown up. A far cry from Della's own childhood home—not quite a slum, but only one step up.

Her own parents were blue-collar working class. Occasionally. Most of the time they were lazy slobs, and Della could hardly believe she possessed any of their genes. They'd hated her friendship with Lyn and the 'big ideas' it had given her. What was so crazy about going to university and getting a well-paid job? She'd shown them, hadn't she?

She sighed. Even now, when they'd gone from her life for good, she still felt she had something to prove—she just didn't know what.

As a teenager, she'd spent every spare minute at Lyn's house. She loved it. It was a happy home. Not just because the Brayfords had money, but because Dawn and Frank Brayford had a genuine interest in their children. And they'd treated her like one of them. She'd had more support and encouragement from the Brayfords than she'd ever had from her folks.

After parking in the street outside the Brayford family home, Della sat for a moment, gathering her defences. Luke wouldn't be there yet, so she had nothing to fear. Not that she feared Luke. It was her own emotions that frightened her.

Thirteen years. Had it really been so long since he'd left Adelaide to take up his dream job? Why hadn't her feelings diminished in all that time? She'd expected to get over him. She'd intended to. But here she was, thirteen years later, feeling her stomach swish at the prospect of seeing him again.

It was hard to believe he was coming home to live. Settling down wasn't in his nature or, at least, it never had been. Maybe this was his wife's doing; although she hadn't seemed the type to want Luke's parents involved in her life.

Della wondered whether Lyn had got the wrong end of the stick. Or maybe Dawn, in her excitement, had read too much into his words. This was just another visit, surely?

But then it crossed Della's mind that he and his wife might be starting a family. The thought twisted her insides. Her stomach tried to squeeze its way into her throat.

She breathed. Deep, slow breaths.

In that case, the move was not so difficult to understand. Adelaide was the perfect place to raise a family. And, if it turned out she was right, she'd just have to get on with her life. She could do it, even if it tore her apart inside.

Calmer, she climbed out of the Mercedes sports car, locking the door, though in this locality it didn't stand out. Luxury cars were the norm rather than the exception.

Not prone to whims, she prided herself on carefully considering a financial commitment—any kind of commitment—but the car had taken her by surprise. In an unguarded moment, she'd fallen hopelessly in love. One look, one touch and she'd been hooked.

With a rueful smile she admitted it had been just the same with Luke, then she straightened her shoulders and turned into the front garden.

Lyn opened the front door. 'You should see the kitchen,' she said with a shake of her head. 'Mum's trying to make every one of Luke's favourite dishes. I know it'll be great to see him, but honestly...'

As Della entered the house, Lyn jerked a thumb towards a door off the spacious foyer. 'Come into the lounge. I've made you a drink like I promised.'

'Perhaps I should offer to help Dawn?' Della flicked an uncertain glance towards the kitchen door.

'Uh-uh.' Lyn tugged at her arm. 'She wants to spoil her favourite son, and the best thing we can do is leave her to it.'

Della allowed Lyn to drag her into the comfortable lounge. As she sat on ૭ sofa, Lyn handed her the biggest margarita she'd ever seen.

'Where did you find this glass? Are you sure it's not a vase?'

Lyn shrugged. 'If it is, it's one of a matching pair.' She picked up its mate and took a sip. 'Mmm. I make a mean margarita.'

Della sipped and had to agree. Just enough lime to make her tongue curl, and plenty of tequila.

'I know you don't want to talk about the doc now,' Lyn said, lowering herself cautiously onto the low sofa opposite, drink in hand. 'But I want you to know, I'm here for you when you're ready. Any time. Day or night. I'm usually up with Cassie anyway.'

'I know, and I will talk to you, but I need time to take it in first. What about a night out this week? We can talk and eat.'

'Excellent idea. I'll check when Patrick can watch the kids. I'll try for tomorrow night.' Her face creased with concern. 'Will that be too soon?'

Della shook her head. Hopefully, she'd have a few minutes to herself in the next twenty-four hours. Quiet time to think. To accept.

A wail reached them. 'Bummer,' Lyn said with a sigh. 'Cassie's awake and right on cue. I hoped she'd sleep through dinner.'

'Where's Jamie?'

'With Dad in his den, looking at model planes. I'd better go and see to Cassie.'

Della watched her leave, before placing her drink on an end table and taking the opportunity to nip into the nearest bathroom. Fixing her make-up, she thought for the millionth time that she was lucky to have Lyn as her friend. She'd always felt that way. Ever since the day at the beach when they'd been fourteen and Lyn had come to her rescue, paying for the fish and chips Della had ordered before finding she didn't have enough money for them. Rigid with embarrassment, she'd stood by while Lyn had stepped in, paid for her order, insisted on buying her a cold drink, and stayed by her side for the rest of the day.

Della shook her head. That day was as clear to her as if it had happened yesterday. Lyn probably didn't even remember it.

Before parting from her new friend, Della had made a careful note of her address, intending to repay her as soon as she could scrape together the money. But, when she'd finally made it, she'd stood at the wrought-iron gate, too scared to press down on the heavy catch.

Then Luke had arrived. To her, he'd seemed much more than one year older. He had such a physical presence even then. Muscular from playing football. Tall. Of course, it didn't help that she was such a tiny thing. He'd towered over her and would have scared her if not for his smile. That mind-melting, breath-stealing, knee-weakening smile.

Della sighed and tossed the make-up into her bag. Emerging from the bathroom, she heard a commotion near the front door.

'It's a taxi. It's them!'

Della recognised the voice as Lyn's younger sister, Megan. Poppy, the baby of the family at twenty-five, called to her mother and Dawn's excited voice joined the mix.

Della didn't go to them. Time for family. Real family. As inclusive as they'd always been, she wasn't real family. Back in the lounge, she picked up her glass and made for the French doors which opened to an expansive deck. She leaned on the waist-high balustrade and sipped her drink while gazing down on the established garden. Dense shrubs screened out the neighbours, and low-growing plants packed the curving flower beds. She'd always loved this garden. So different from the weed-infested lawn and corrugated fencing of her parents' place. She soaked up the sense of peace the garden offered. She needed it more than ever.

'There you are, Shrimp.'

Della gave a violent start, sending a minor flood of margarita onto the lawn below. Luke's deep and teasing voice was unmistakeable. It had the same effect on her it always had, making her nerves jump to attention, ready to react to every provocative word he said. She turned.

Oh God, he looked amazing. The last time she'd seen him, his dark-blond hair had been short, but he'd changed jobs since then and his hair had grown past his collar. More like the young Luke. Casual. She guessed appearances didn't matter so much now he wasn't on TV any more.

His smile widened as he observed the so-called glass in her hand. Her hand tightened, as did her stomach. That killer smile had no doubt served him well. Even a hardened, gun-toting rebel couldn't refuse an interview when faced with such a smile.

His warm grey eyes twinkled as he raised them to her face. 'You must be thirsty,' he said.

Suppressing the urge to fling herself at him, she shrugged. 'Stress relief,' she said, regretting the words the moment they left her lips. Even more so when he frowned.

'A hard day at work,' she said quickly.

His frown deepened. 'Don't you like your job?'

'Yes, of course I do. You don't need me to tell you work can be stressful, no matter how much you enjoy it.'

He should know if anyone did. For ten years as a foreign correspondent, he'd travelled the world's hot spots, mainly in Asia, covering stories of conflict and disaster. He'd pioneered solo-journalism, working completely alone, travelling and reporting without a crew, carrying a backpack of portable digital technology to shoot, write, edit and transmit multimedia reports. He hadn't chased headlines or taken part in pack journalism, but had specialised in pursuing stories that were not getting main-stream news coverage and putting a human face to them.

Della lifted the glass and gulped a mouthful of margarita. Too much. When she'd managed to swallow it, she said, 'Well, anyway, what about you? How are you?'

'Fine.' He watched her for a moment. 'So where's my kiss? My hug? I've had them from everyone else. I haven't been around for a while, in case you haven't noticed.'

'Oh. Yes.' Leaning forward, she gave him an awkward, one-armed hug while she held the glass well out of the way.

He hugged her back, tighter than necessary. She could feel the heat of his body through his shirt, and a heat of a different kind rushed through her own body. It reminded her what it was like to be—to *feel*—attracted to a man. Then he kissed her on the cheek. She pulled away in a hurry.

His grin gave her the impression he knew why. But he couldn't. There'd never been anything physical between them. Never. Not even the suggestion of an attraction. He couldn't possibly know.

She let her gaze slide over his face. His nose still had the slight kink in the middle from the time Lyn had dared him to skateboard down a handrail. Lyn had blamed herself when he'd landed face-first on the concrete steps. She should have known better than to issue a challenge to Luke. He'd never backed away from a challenge. Not then. Not later.

He intercepted her gaze and held it. 'You look great, Shrimp. Not a day older than when I first left.'

She couldn't say the same for him. The dangerous and outdoor life he'd led had added plenty of lines around his eyes. Lines that creased deeply when he smiled. But that wasn't a bad thing. Age had added character to a face she would once have called perfect.

She gave a tiny snort. 'Don't they have opticians where you've been living?'

He ignored her question. 'I like what you've done with your hair. Short suits you. It's sophisticated.'

'For a shrimp?'

'It wasn't short last time I came over, was it?'

'No, I only had it cut recently.' Not that he'd have noticed on that trip three years ago, she thought. He'd had eyes for no one but his new wife. She doubted her own presence had even registered with him.

He hadn't shaved in a while, probably on account of the long flight. On him, the look wasn't so much scruffy as sexy. Her nerve endings twitched again. Her reaction to Luke contrasted sharply with the antipathy she'd felt for the men she'd dated over the last few years. She'd almost had to force herself to take a physical interest, and had begun to think she wasn't capable of it. This was a bad time to find out she was.

Suddenly feeling overdressed in her business suit next to Luke's torn jeans and battered denim jacket, her eyes widened. 'Is that the same jacket you had when we were kids?'

He nodded. 'I wondered if you'd recognise it.'

'Your job must pay poorly if you can't afford some decent clothes.' Since he'd given up the journalism and taken up running an orphanage, she guessed he'd taken a big drop in salary. But he would never be poor. His grandfather had left a trust fund that would see him through.

He shrugged. 'I won't part with this jacket. It has sentimental value.'

She gave him a sceptical look, and he laughed. 'Plus, it's comfortable.'

'And comfort clearly ranks highly in your world. Why else would you hike through the mountains of Afghanistan—?'

'Now Luke, you're not teasing Della, are you?'

Della turned towards Dawn as she joined them on the deck.

'We had enough of these games when you were kids,' Dawn said.

'Actually, I've complimented her new hairstyle.' He slid an arm around his mother's waist and hugged her to his side. 'But she doesn't believe she looks gorgeous.'

Dawn beamed up at him. 'I don't blame her, considering how you used to torment her. But it is lovely, isn't it?' She turned back to study Della. 'I think it makes her look like Audrey Hepburn.'

'As if.' Della laughed. 'You're deluded, Dawn. And you, Luke, are the last person I'd believe.'

She was proud of herself. She sounded cool, calm and collected. No one would guess she felt the complete opposite. No one would know she'd spent more than half her life comparing every man who'd come near her with this one, rejecting every one of them because they fell short of her ideal.

'I thought you were bringing Yvonne with you,' Dawn said to Luke. 'You haven't left her back in India, have you?'

Luke's gaze slid away for a moment. When he looked back, his expression was blank.

'Yes, she's still there as far as I know. I'll explain when we're all together.'

Curiosity sparked in Dawn's eyes. 'Well, let's eat,' she said. 'Come through to the dining room.'

As they took their places around the large oak dining-table, Della wished she really did belong to this family. This was what she'd always wanted for her own children—a home filled with warmth and laughter.

She looked down, spreading the linen napkin across her lap and fighting the sting in her eyes.

No chance of that now.

CHAPTER TWO

'ARE you really home to stay?' Poppy said through a mouthful of salad.

Luke looked at his little sister. He found it hard to believe that she'd grown up so much since he'd last seen her. 'How many times do I have to say it?' he said with feigned exasperation.

'Yeah, I know, but *really?*' Poppy said. 'Won't you be bored?'

Luke shrugged. 'Don't think so.'

'But there are no wars around here. Nothing bad ever happens in Adelaide.'

'Thank God for it,' Dawn said. 'We are very lucky to live in one of the safest cities on earth. I should think Luke's had quite enough of war and poverty and the like. If he has the sense he was born with, he'll want to stay well away from all of that.'

He smiled at his mother. She'd never missed an opportunity to tell him he was crazy for choosing to make his home where he had. But she'd never criticised him either. Though she couldn't understand his choices, she'd always respected his right to make them.

Both his parents had. His gaze drifted to his father. His salt-and-pepper hair was now almost all salt. He hoped he hadn't caused him too much worry over the years.

Next to their father, his sister Megan was deep in discus-

sion with their brother-in-law, Patrick. It seemed Lyn's
marriage had not only survived, but thrived. His gaze moved
on to Lyn, the baby in her arms and her son at her side. His
niece and nephew. He'd have time to get to know them better
now, and he fully intended to.

Skinny Lynnie, as he'd always called her, had gained
weight. It suited her. She caught his eye and gave him a
cheeky wink. He grinned back. So close in age, they'd been
more like best friends than brother and sister. All three of
them, in fact. His gaze shifted to Della, the third member of
their little gang.

If he thought his sisters had changed, he couldn't find words
to describe the transformation in Della. She was still small and
slender, but more confident. More sure of herself and her
appeal. She looked...serene. As if nothing could ruffle her.
And she exuded femininity. Her beautifully cut, very short hair
showed off great cheekbones, and he liked the way her neck
curved above the collar of her business jacket. In the past, it
had been hidden by a swathe of long, dark hair which had often
fallen across her face. A shield between her and the world.

She must have grown out of her shyness to have cut her
hair. Well, it had never really been shyness. More like embarrassment for who she was and where she'd come from.

Della lifted her head to look at Lyn and her eyes nearly
knocked him out. Large, dark and slightly slanted. She'd ac-
centuated their shape with make-up, and he had to admit her
eyes were a striking feature without the long hair obscuring
them.

He continued to watch her, couldn't bring himself to look
away. She smiled as she chatted to Lyn, fussed over Jamie,
teased Poppy. But her eyes... They didn't smile. He could
almost believe she was sad. But why, when she seemed to
have everything going for her?

Not grieving for her parents, surely? They didn't deserve

a second thought from her. His gut tightened. A whole raft of memories came flooding back. Amongst other things, he remembered his mother taking Della to the doctor and telling him later that Della's small size was a result of malnutrition during her formative years.

In recent times, he'd seen plenty of children suffering from malnutrition, and it made his blood boil to think it had happened to Della and here, in Australia, one of the more affluent countries in the world. He knew his own parents had considered initiating adoption proceedings, but something must have gone wrong. They would have adopted her if they could.

As he watched her, Della smiled down at Jamie. When her lips parted and she moistened them with the tip of her tongue, Luke experienced a subtle shift in his stomach. It felt a lot like sexual attraction, but it couldn't be.

'So what are you going to do, son?'

Luke jerked his gaze from Della and leaned back in his chair as he focused on his father. 'About what?'

'Work.'

He smiled. 'I've had a job offer.'

'You have?' Frank mopped at his mouth with his napkin.

He nodded. 'It's not finalised yet, so I don't want to say much about it, but it's with the charity I've been working for in India.'

'And it's here in Adelaide?'

'Yes.'

A clatter drew Luke's eyes to Della again, and he saw her cheeks grow pink as she retrieved her fork from the floor.

'Talking of jobs, Shrimp, when are you going to desert the enemy?'

The colour in her cheeks deepened. 'Enemy?'

'Okay, enemy is a bit strong.' He shrugged. 'But you public relations people, you're the gatekeepers. The ones who stop hard-working journos like me from getting at the nitty gritty.'

She frowned. 'Without PR people like me, you journos would have to work a hell of a lot harder. We do most of the work for you by providing all the information you need.'

'All the information you want us to have, you mean.'

'Without us, you'd have to get off your backsides and look for the stories yourselves.' She felt a stab of guilt at using this old argument against Luke, who could never be accused of taking the easy way out. He was far removed from that type, but she was on the defensive. She went on. She couldn't help herself.

'The vast majority of items in the news have been initiated by PR, whether in-house specialists or external consultants—'

'Oh, I admit there are some lazy journos around. Some of them should be ashamed of themselves. They regurgitate a press release and put their by-line on it. No, I'm referring to those of us who care about getting at the truth, and who find our way blocked by PR people tidying up the messes left by their corporate clients.'

'Now, now, Luke,' Dawn said, wagging a finger at him. 'You know he doesn't mean it, Della. He's trying to get you to bite, like he always did. Ignore him.' She turned back to Luke. 'Della is very good at her job so you leave her alone. She's in line for a big promotion, too. Very highly thought of, our Della.'

'And you're not even a journalist any more,' Lyn piped up. 'You haven't been for what, three years?'

He smiled. 'But I'm still allowed to defend the profession.'

His mother was half right. Though he did enjoy teasing Della, he was semi-serious. He didn't like to think of her on the side of some of the corporate creeps he'd encountered over the years. But this wasn't the time or place to bring that subject up. He grinned at Della, and her lovely mouth gave him an answering smile before she turned away to help Jamie cut his meat.

'You said you would explain about Yvonne,' Dawn said. 'Is she travelling alone? Or will you be going back for her? What's going on?'

'Ah.' He took a mouthful of wine and let the rich, fruity flavour swirl around his mouth before swallowing. He put down the glass and leaned his elbows on the table, linking his hands. 'I'm afraid I have some news. Yvonne and I have broken up. She won't be coming here.' He shrugged. 'I don't know where she is right now, and to be honest I don't care.'

He looked down at his plate while a silence settled over the table, each person absorbing his news. His grip tightened. It wasn't news to him but it was still difficult to talk about.

'You're getting divorced?' his mother asked eventually.

'Yes. It's already underway.'

'But this is so sudden. Your last email said you were both fine.'

He grimaced. 'Well, we were. We just weren't together. I'm sorry I didn't tell you, but it's been over for a while.'

'Have you tried counselling?'

'No.' He snorted. 'Believe me, there's no point.'

'Oh, Luke. What happened? You were so in love. I remember thinking when you brought Yvonne to meet us that I'd never seen you so happy.'

'Mum, I'd rather not go into the details. We weren't meant to be together. That's all there is to it. Just accept it's over, okay?'

Dawn hesitated. 'Of course, but I'm so sorry. Still, if it had to happen, it's a blessing you didn't have any children.'

Luke's jaw clenched, a muscle twitched. 'I don't consider that a blessing.'

With a sigh, he reached for his glass and drank the remaining wine. He hadn't intended to go there. He didn't want to expose his emotions to the scrutiny of others, even his family, as much as he loved them.

His mother broke the tense silence. 'Where are your bags? Did you leave them at the airport?'

'No, they're at the hotel. I checked in on the way here.'

'Hotel? Why would you want to stay at a hotel when you have a perfectly good room here?'

'I didn't want to put you to the trouble, especially as I sprung my visit on you.'

'Rubbish. What's this house for if not for our family? Check out of the hotel tomorrow and move in here. You need to be where we can look after you.'

Luke smiled, but shook his head. He didn't need or want looking after. He'd managed on his own for years. He was used to it. If his marriage had taught him anything, it was that he was better off alone.

Later, instead of lingering over coffee and home-made chocolate mints as she was tempted to do, Della pushed back her chair. 'I'm sorry to rush off, but I have to do some work tonight.'

'Work?' Dawn asked. 'You work too hard. Are you sure you have to?'

'Afraid so,' she said. 'We have a crisis we're dealing with at the moment.'

'Not the Dermont Chemicals fire?' Frank said. 'I heard about it on the radio.'

She nodded. 'That's the one. Tom Dermont is my client. Lucky me.'

'I hope they appreciate how much you do after hours,' Dawn said. 'But I doubt it.'

Luke leapt from his seat. 'Hey, you can give me a lift,' he said. 'Just into the city. Okay?'

Damn. Work was only part of the reason she had to leave.

She needed to get away from Luke. The effort of pretending not to care had made her chest ache. The news of his divorce had made it worse, and she wasn't sure which was stronger—sympathy for his obvious pain or relief that he was free again. She felt shamed that it might be relief.

'Um, do you really want to leave so soon?' Della glanced at Dawn, hoping she'd press him to stay longer.

'I expect you're exhausted after all the travelling,' Dawn said, rising to give her son a hug.

So much for that idea. In the confusion of goodbye hugs and kisses, Della slipped out to the car. Her head was spinning with all she'd heard. Not only his divorce, but the fact he'd be living and working here in Adelaide.

Not that any of it made a difference to her position. On the contrary, she was as determined as ever to keep her feelings hidden. She wouldn't risk ruining a friendship she valued when he was clearly hurting and needing his friends. Once she'd absorbed everything that had happened today and had a good night's sleep, she'd be ready, willing and able to be his friend. Though he hadn't admitted it, and maybe he didn't even know it, she was sure a big part of his homecoming was a need for emotional support.

'Thought you'd left without me,' Luke said as he opened the passenger door and slid in. 'Nice car. *Very* nice. You have good taste, Shrimp.'

She started the engine of the silver convertible. 'What did you think I'd have—a Volvo? Nice and safe?'

He laughed. 'I can't say I've ever thought about it, but if I had I'd have pegged you as having a…Mini.'

'A Mini!'

'A shrimp car.'

'Oh, shut up.'

'Nice driving,' he commented after a few moments.

'Thanks.' She enjoyed driving. It was one of the things she

was good at. Which probably explained why she'd been lured by the car.

'So, what happened to your ideals, Della?'

'My ideals?'

'The ones we talked about when we were at university. You were just as keen to fix the world as I was.'

'I was young and silly and thought I knew everything.'

'Now you're old and silly and know you know nothing?'

She gave him a sideways glance. 'Something like that.' She'd never been as focused as Luke. She'd admired the strength of his convictions, but had been more interested in creating a firm financial foundation for herself than in changing a world that didn't want to be changed. 'Where do you want me to drop you?'

He stared at their surroundings for a moment. 'North Terrace,' he said, before turning back to face her. 'It would be good to catch up. It's been a while since we hung out together.'

She heard a wistful undertone. 'A while? It's been *ages*.'

'You're not wrong. What about tomorrow? You could skip work for a day.'

'I wish I could but I have a crisis, remember?'

'Ah, yes. Dermont's. A shining example of corporate social responsibility. Tomorrow night?'

She shook her head. 'I'm going out with Lyn. Hopefully.'

'Hopefully?'

'If Patrick can watch the kids.'

'The night after, then?'

'I'll have to keep it open in case Lyn needs to reschedule.'

She focused on manoeuvring the car into the kerb. It wasn't a good place to stop, and he opened the door without delay.

'Thanks,' he said over his shoulder. 'Have a good night.'

As soon as he closed the door, she set off towards the sea and her haven. Though she tried not to, she glanced repeatedly at her rear-view mirror, searching for a final glimpse of him before he disappeared from sight. It had taken all her energy to keep up the pretence tonight. She didn't remember it being so difficult on his previous visits.

Just for an instant, she wondered if there was a chance she'd ever be able to reveal her true feelings. Now he was divorced and home to stay, what was there to stop her?

Friendship.

He'd been head over heels when he'd brought Yvonne to meet his family. Besotted. She wouldn't be surprised if he still loved her. If so, the last thing he needed was Della confessing her secrets and adding to his confusion.

For now that was true, but what about the future?

She clamped down on the thought. She had no business thinking about the future when she'd already accepted her priority was to be a friend to Luke.

But could they pick up their friendship where they'd left off? Or would there be a distance between them that hadn't existed before he'd gone overseas?

On his brief visits back home, he'd been elusive, distracted. Passing through, nothing more. Thinking about his last story, his next story, not staying in one spot long enough to talk or, as he put it, hang out. Later, the one and only time he'd brought his wife home, he'd had no time or thought for anyone but Yvonne.

They had heaps of catching up to do. A hell of a lot had happened in his life. But a great deal had happened to her too, and nothing she wanted to discuss. Just for starters, her illness and its consequences would be off-limits. Even with him back, and apparently ready to settle down, things could never be quite the same as before.

The next morning, Della awoke with a headache. A certain smile had invaded her dreams, wrecking the small amount of sleep she'd had. After showering and dressing, she felt almost human. Despite the headache, she did feel better than she had the night before. She poured a glass of orange juice and made her way out to the front verandah from where she had a panoramic view of Gulf St Vincent. A rich turquoise sea met a deep blue, cloudless spring sky.

A small public lawn area separated her front garden from the sandy beach. The road didn't reach this far, a leftover from the days when the heritage-listed house had been built. She eased herself into the swing-seat suspended from the iron framework of the verandah and sipped the chilled juice while she thought about the previous day.

If Luke was going to be living and working here, she wouldn't be able to avoid him. Nor did she want to. Given the choice between never seeing him again, or loving him and having to hide it, she'd choose to put herself through the agony of being near him. Of course she would.

She'd learned as a child that it was not only possible but essential to conceal the truth if it would do no good to display it. This didn't make her dishonest, just very good at burying her feelings.

Last night had confirmed she was as strongly attracted to Luke now as ever but, more important than that, she was Luke's oldest friend. As far as she knew, he hadn't kept in touch with any of his old mates from school or footy. And if he needed to talk about his marriage break-up, his oldest friend had a duty to be there for him. And she would.

If he still loved his wife—and she suspected he did—he'd be suffering dreadfully. She'd certainly seen flashes of pain cross his eyes when he'd broken the news to his family. He was the type to make light of his feelings, so the fact he hadn't been able to hide how much he hurt made her heart ache for him.

If it would help him to talk about Yvonne, she'd listen. The next time he asked her to hang out, she wouldn't make excuses. She'd force her feelings back into their box and do what she had to do.

Raucous squawks from seagulls drew her head up, and she watched the birds circling for a minute before she stood to go inside. Much as she'd like to stay, she had no time to waste. She had a media conference to organise.

On the way from the basement car park to her office, Della stopped by Reception to greet Bonnie and check for messages.

Bonnie, framed by floral arrangements, sat behind a curved jarrah desk. 'Hi, Della. Marvin's been looking for you.'

'Already? Is he in his office?'

'Mmm. Jason's in there too.'

'Is he?' Neither her boss, Marvin, nor her assistant could claim to be early starters. This crisis must have freaked them. She hurried to drop a pile of files on her desk, plonked down her briefcase and handbag, then headed along the passageway to Marvin's corner office. With no sign of his secretary, Della knocked on his door and entered.

'Here she is,' Marvin said, consulting his watch. 'Della, we have a problem with this media conference today.'

'A problem?' She took a seat next to Jason, who flashed her a brief smile.

'Tom Dermont rang me at home this morning. Apparently, your mobile was switched off.' He raised his eyebrows.

'I had a headache—'

'Never mind that now.' He waved a hand in front of his face as if swatting her words away. 'The point is, he wants to front the media.'

Della closed her eyes. 'Dear God.'

'Exactly. What the—?' He ran a finger around his shirt collar. 'What the flaming heck are you going to do about it?'

Stifling her gut reaction to panic, she took a deep breath. 'I'll talk to him, Marvin,' she said in a level voice.

'Talk to him? You'll need a jackhammer to get through his thick skull.' He glanced at the door, as if afraid he'd been overheard. 'Do it quickly. And let me know how it goes.' He picked up his phone and Della stood to leave.

'Don't worry, Marvin,' Jason said. 'I'll help her.'

Della turned on her heel, her eyebrows rising in disbelief. The nerve of him. She would have made it clear she didn't require his assistance if Marvin hadn't already begun his phone conversation. She strode towards the door, and he scuttled across the office behind her.

In the passageway, Jason dashed in front and barred her way. 'Don't want you to get the wrong idea, Della,' he said. 'I was only trying to help. Didn't mean to make it sound like you couldn't handle it.'

No, of course he hadn't. Not in front of her, anyway. Out of her hearing was a different matter. He'd been laying the groundwork for his advancement for the past six months. And she wouldn't have a problem with him taking her position, as long as he waited for her to vacate the office before moving in.

If things went to plan, and she won the promotion to partner as expected, it would work in her favour to have a ready-made replacement. She wouldn't hesitate to recommend Jason in that case. If, however, he continued to make snide comments like the one she'd just witnessed, she might suggest the company look elsewhere for its new senior consultant.

Ignoring his squirms, she got down to business. 'Start making up the media kits,' she said. 'I emailed the media release to you late last night. Have you seen it?'

'Haven't checked my in-box yet.'

'Well, do so. You should have everything else you need on file. Also, contact Catherine and tell her we need an employee communication plan. I'll get in touch with Tom Dermont.'

'Do you want me—?'

'I can handle him,' she said curtly.

'Of course.'

She dismissed him with a flick of her wrist and walked back to her office. With a sigh, she walked around her desk. She didn't enjoy acting the heavy-handed boss, but she knew his sort, and wasn't naïve enough to believe another way existed. She'd had to be tough to reach this level in the firm and she'd have to be tougher still if she made it to partner. Though it didn't come naturally to her, a certain amount of ruthlessness was essential.

A message waited on the desk. She picked up the slip of yellow paper as she slid into her chair. Melanie Crowe, the in-house PR officer employed by Dermont Chemicals. Couldn't be good news. She'd better deal with Melanie's problem first before tackling Tom.

Melanie was out of her depth in this type of crisis, and Della felt sorry for her. Tom had tried to cut costs by hiring a green graduate rather than an older, experienced practitioner.

If Tom had any real business sense, he'd put his money into developing a less confrontational relationship with the local residents and preparing emergency plans for incidents such as yesterday's fire. They'd still need to bring in consultants for the legwork and logistical management, but at least they wouldn't have journalists filling their stories with hearsay and uninformed comments.

It wasn't in her interests to suggest this, though. The firm made a tidy sum from Dermont's contract, and as he wouldn't—

or couldn't—work with anyone but her it put her in a strong position with the senior partners.

'Melanie, you called.'

'Oh, Della. Thank goodness.' Melanie answered sounding breathless, and it was only eight-thirty in the morning. 'It's escalating,' she said.

'I thought the fire brigade had it under control.'

'They did, but then it reached one of the chemical storage tanks and there was an explosion. Oh, hell, two firefighters are in hospital.'

'Badly hurt?'

'Stable. Thing is, toxic fumes are leaking. The police are evacuating the locals.'

Della swore under her breath. This was the last thing they needed—more ammunition for the residents' protest group. If they could convince the state government the chemical plant should be reclassified as heavy industrial, Dermont's would be forced to move operations to the outer suburbs, well away from residential areas. Such a move would cost Dermont's a fortune, and could even mean the end of their operations if Tom Dermont decided to pull the plug and cut his losses.

'Thanks for letting me know, Melanie. I'm going to speak to Tom now. He wants to run the media conference, and I need to talk him out of it.'

Melanie snorted. 'Good luck.'

'I thought I'd suggest Dan Barlow as the ideal person to take his place.'

'Perfect. He'll come across as a good guy. Plus, he knows what he's talking about. He won't try to bluster his way through like Tom would.'

That afternoon, Della flicked through one of the media kits Jason had piled on a table near the entrance to the large room. As well as her media release, he'd included background details on the Dermont products, a piece on the company's contribution to the state economy, a fact sheet regarding a proposed project to clean up the production process—if Tom Dermont ever approved the expenditure—and other bits and pieces. They'd hired a large conference room at a city hotel and sent out the media advisory notes. Now all she could do was hope Tom stayed away as he'd promised in their phone call.

Dan Barlow entered the room, and she hurried over to him. 'Thanks for agreeing to do this, Dan,' she said.

'Not a problem. Glad to help.'

She chatted to Dan for several moments then, as she swung around, doing a speedy check of chairs available for the stream of media representatives coming through the door, she spotted Luke. He caught her eye as he took a seat in the back row, and his smile made her empty stomach go into freefall. She made her way to the back of the room.

'What are you doing here?' she asked, standing close behind his chair.

He twisted to face her. His gaze drifted from the top of her head to her toes and back up to her face. A blatant inspection. She had to stop herself gasping out loud. He'd never looked at her like this before.

'I like the way you dress for work,' he said. 'Very smart, but not too corporate. There's still a touch of the old Della there.'

Absurdly pleased, she smoothed down her tailored black skirt, straightened her silk shirt and lifted her chin. 'I'm glad to see an improvement in *your* clothes.'

In fact, he looked incredible, treading the line between smart and casual in his olive-green combat trousers and a white, short-sleeved shirt. Clean-shaven, he'd also had a haircut.

'You haven't said what you're doing here,' she said.

'Just checking out the local news scene.'

'You're not working, are you?'

He shook his head.

'Then, how did you even know this was happening?'

He hesitated. 'I still have contacts in the local media.'

'Oh. Of course.' She glanced at her watch. Running late was not an option with the evening news crews facing broadcast deadlines. 'I'd better go. Time to start.'

'Sure. See you tonight.'

'Not tonight. I'm going out with Lyn, remember?'

He nodded.

Della walked calmly to the front of the room. She should have known he wouldn't be able to stay away from a media conference like this. Renowned all over the world for his hard-hitting exposés of exploitation and corporate greed, he was a media favourite here in his home town. Of course he still had contacts, and as soon as he got in touch they'd fill him in on the biggest story of the day.

She glanced Luke's way from time to time—and each time she did he caught her. A raised eyebrow, a wink, a cheeky half-smile. She had to force herself not to look in his direction again or she'd burst out laughing and wreck the media conference, not to mention her own reputation as a self-possessed professional.

She lost sight of him in the mass exodus, and by the time she'd dealt with the debriefing, prepared the action plan for the next few days and returned to her office, the adrenalin high she'd been on all day started to subside. She scanned the messages strewn across her desk, and sighed when she spotted one from a client in the wine industry. She'd have to delegate the remaining work on their annual report or it wouldn't be ready in time for the printing deadline.

Her mobile phone beeped and she read the text message on the screen:

ok for tonight. be here @ 6. lyn

With mixed feelings, she cleared the screen. She enjoyed any time spent with Lyn, but tonight was going to be tough.

CHAPTER THREE

DELLA drove to Lyn's house. She'd put in a superhuman effort, clearing a mountain of work so she could leave without a guilty conscience. When she reached Lyn's, she saw an unfamiliar car parked in the driveway. A Saab. Visitors? Would Lyn be obliged to stay home? Della almost hoped she would. Almost. But that would be the coward's way out, and she was no coward.

She rang the doorbell. Lyn flung open the door, Cassie cradled in her arms. 'I'm nearly ready,' she said before Della could speak. 'Here, take Cassie and I'll finish my make-up.'

Della cuddled Cassie into her shoulder. Assuming the car belonged to one of Patrick's friends, she headed through a door off the hallway. She came to an abrupt stop when she saw Luke sitting on the floor, playing a game with Jamie.

'Hi.' He looked up, giving her a wry smile. 'Want to play?'

She tried to squash the excitement bubbling up at seeing him again, and shook her head. 'Just waiting for Lyn. I expected to see Patrick.'

'He had to work. I offered to babysit.'

'You? Babysit?'

'Don't look so shocked. It will give me an opportunity to get to know my cheating nephew better.' He tweaked Jamie's nose. 'And my beautiful niece.' He reached up and jiggled one dangling foot as Cassie snuggled further into Della's shoulder. 'Besides,' he said, 'I couldn't have you putting me off indefinitely and using Patrick as an excuse.'

She blinked. 'Right.'

He must really need to talk if he'd gone to this trouble to make sure she'd be free. She had better be prepared for the floodgates to open.

Jamie demanded his attention, and he answered the little boy patiently. It shouldn't surprise her. He'd been good with Megan and Poppy when they'd been little. But somehow the scene cut right to her core, causing a sharp ache deep inside.

He looked up. 'So, dinner tomorrow night, then? Shall I pick you up? I have a car now.'

'The Saab outside? You bought it?'

'Yup. Like it? I decided to treat myself. I've never had a decent car. Tell you what, we could eat at your place. Don't worry about cooking, I'll bring dinner and wine.'

She was still stuck on the fact he'd bought a car. He really was settling down. Next thing she knew, he'd be buying a house. 'Sorry, what?'

'I said, I'll bring food and we'll eat at your place. You're still a burger freak, I assume?'

She nodded.

'Ready?' Lyn called from the doorway.

'I'll be there at seven,' he said.

'What's this?' Lyn asked. 'You two going out without me?'

'Lynnie, you wrecked our gang when you married Patrick. Now you have to suffer the consequences,' Luke said.

She pouted. 'Well, just you look after my kids, Uncle Luke. Come on, Della, let's leave him to it. I've given them both prunes for tea, so he'll have a lovely time.'

Della grinned at the look of horror on Luke's face as she handed Cassie to him.

'Not really,' Lyn mouthed as she shut the door behind them.

Mamma Marcella's, their restaurant of choice, was busier than normal, but they found a table in the back corner near the kitchen. Della liked the relaxed ambience, and the owners let them linger long after they'd finished coffee. The perfect place for a catch-up chat.

They ordered at the counter and bought drinks before settling at their table.

'Right. I've been a very patient friend, but I'm dying to know. What did the doctor say?'

Della steeled herself. She knew she had to talk about it. She might as well get it over with early then she could relax for the rest of the evening.

Relax? Ha! She didn't know the meaning of the word.

'It's definite,' she said. 'As suspected, I can't have children.'

'Oh, Della.' Lyn's face contorted. 'I'm so sorry. Are they sure? Is there nothing they can do?'

Della shook her head, swallowing past the cricket ball in her throat.

'IVF?' Lyn suggested tentatively.

'No. She said the ovarian follicles won't respond to the stimulation.'

'Bugger, bugger, bugger.' Lyn took a gulp from her glass. 'It's so unfair.'

Della shrugged, trying for casual. 'I always knew the chemo could do this.'

'I know, but there was hope. Until now.' Lyn took another deep drink. 'God, I can only imagine how you feel.' She gave her friend a long look. 'How *do* you feel?'

Della took a moment to choose her words. 'I feel...diminished.'

'Oh, my God. No.' Lyn squeezed Della's hand.

'I don't even understand why I feel this way,' Della rushed on. 'I mean, it's not like I'm planning to get married in the foreseeable future, and chances are I never will.'

'Don't say that.'

'Why not? It's a fact.' She paused, dragging in a deep breath and making an effort to slow down. If she allowed herself to gabble, the next thing she knew she'd be in tears. Slowing her speech always helped her to appear calm.

'The point is,' she said, 'it was a fact before I saw Dr Morgan, and I didn't feel any less a person then.'

'Nor should you now. There's no reason why you shouldn't find a man to marry. A man who doesn't want children. I mean, the right man. Not like those losers you've dated over the last few years.'

'Losers? They weren't all losers.' Okay, some were. But as for the others, well, it wasn't their fault she couldn't love them. It was hers.

Lyn gazed at her for several moments. 'It's strange you've never found anyone. I mean, I fancied myself in love something like half a dozen times before I met Patrick. But you, you've never even considered the possibility, have you? Or, if you have, you've never mentioned it.'

Della looked away. She stared at the menu boards on the wall, but the chalk letters turned to squiggles before her eyes. She'd considered love all right. Very long and very hard. She hadn't wanted to ruin their friendship by telling Lyn she'd fallen in love with her brother all those years ago.

He was so obviously not interested in her as anything but a friend; she hadn't wanted to run the risk of his rejection. God, she could only imagine the mess it would have caused, the awkwardness when she'd gone to Lyn's home. The embarrassment. And Lyn's friendship was so very, very important to her. They were both important to her. What would her life have been like without them? She hadn't wanted to lose either of them. So, her *considered* response had been to hide her feelings.

Her resolve had firmed when she'd realised he wouldn't be sticking around. For a short space of time, she'd suspected he was looking at her in a different way. As if he, too, had been having thoughts that went deeper than friendship. But she'd convinced herself it was just her imagination. And, even if it hadn't been, he'd had so many plans, so much desire to make a difference, such a driving sense of right and wrong.

She would never have put any obstacles in the way of him achieving his goals. Keeping her feelings to herself had been the right thing to do. A relationship with her would have been an obstacle. If he'd stayed, he'd never have felt fulfilled. He'd needed to be completely free to pursue the life he dreamed of. The lonely life of a solo-journalist was what he'd wanted and, because she'd loved him, she'd wanted it for him too.

But now, he'd done it all. And more. She had the evidence, if she needed it, that he'd never had any serious attraction to her. The fact that he'd married Yvonne was proof positive. What she didn't understand was why her own feelings had remained as strong as ever. Despite his marriage, despite the length of time he'd stayed away, she was still in love with him.

'Do you think it's because of your parents?' Lyn asked softly.

Della started. 'My parents?' She narrowed her eyes at her friend, not sure what she was getting at.

'I mean...' Lyn cleared her throat. 'Do you think a lack of affection during your childhood has made it impossible for you to love now? I suppose it's the old question of nature versus nurture, isn't it? How much of our personality is the result of our upbringing, and how much due to innate character?'

Della tilted her head. 'I see what you're saying, but I really don't think… I mean, I'm sure I could love him, if I found the right man.'

Lyn smiled. 'Well, he might be just around the corner,' she said in an encouraging tone.

Della lowered her eyes. Several corners—there were several corners between the restaurant and Lyn's house. She gave her head a slight shake.

Lyn sighed. 'So, if you don't see yourself getting married, what do you think you'll be doing in, say, ten years' time?'

She looked up. This she could answer. She'd given it plenty of thought. 'When I, or rather *if* I get the promotion, I'll be the youngest partner in the firm, as well as the first female. I want to make a success of the role. That will take ten years, easily.'

'Right. Blazing a trail for other women and all that. Hmm, it's all very well, but there's more to life than work, you know.'

A waiter arrived at their table with two plates of food. 'Hi there,' he said. 'Nice to see you back again.'

They both smiled up at him. He was related to the owner, and always had a friendly word for them.

'Enjoy!'

Lyn watched him walk off. 'That is one very cute guy. Pity he's too young for you.'

'Lyn! He's like half my age.'

Lyn laughed. 'He's not that young.' Unwrapping her cutlery, she said, 'I don't want to sound like a broken record, but I do worry about you.'

'You don't need to. I enjoy my work.'

'I don't know why, it always seems so stressful.'

'It's challenging.'

'It's that all right. Sometimes, though, I wonder…'

'Wonder what?'

'How you can work for people like Tom Dermont.'

'Well, not all my clients are like Tom.'

'No, of course not, but he's not the only one like that, either. How do you justify working for them? To yourself? Your conscience?'

Della frowned. 'I don't feel that I have to justify it. I'm not responsible for what he does or doesn't do. It's a job. I only have to concentrate on doing the work to the best of my ability.'

Lyn paused with her fork in mid-air. 'You don't think you'd be happier in a different job?'

Della shook her head.

After chewing her food, Lyn shrugged. 'Anyway, that isn't where I meant to go with this. What I meant was, I don't want you to be so wrapped up in your work that you end up alone.'

'I won't be alone. I have you and Patrick, Jamie and Cassie, Dawn and Frank, Megan and Poppy.'

'And Luke.'

'And...Luke.'

Della averted her eyes, focusing on a young woman who was weaving between the tables, her generous hips swaying. If she was a typical woman, she'd prefer a svelte figure to the wide, childbearing hips she'd been given. But would she give up her chance to have children for it? Very unlikely. Not many women were childless from choice.

'I think,' Della said, 'there's something built into us, you know? Knowing I can't accomplish the basic purpose I was meant for makes me feel less of a woman.'

Lyn's eyes shone and she blinked rapidly. 'I will not have you talking like this. It's nonsense. There are loads of women who don't have children, whether it's a health issue, a life-style thing or otherwise. No one thinks less of them for it. No one will think less of *you*, Dell.'

She nodded. 'Part of me knows you're right, yet it doesn't make a jot of difference to the way I feel. I just need some time to accept it, you know? I need to come to terms with it.

I would have liked…loved—' Her voice cracked and she paused, lips pursed, stomach clenched, willing herself to keep it together. 'To…to have a child of my own some day.'

'Of course, and you'd make—' Lyn bit a trembling lip. 'Would have made a wonderful mother.'

Della fanned her face with her paper napkin. 'Don't tell anyone, Lyn. Don't tell Dawn. I'll explain it to her myself one day, when I'm ready. But not yet.'

Lyn dragged the back of her hand across her eyes. 'Mum will feel badly for you.'

'I know she will. That's the problem. I can't cope with her sympathy yet. I can't cope with anyone's sympathy.' Until she could talk about it without shrivelling up inside, she didn't want anyone else to know.

'Fair enough.' Lyn ducked her head and tugged a tissue from her handbag.

'Let's talk about something else now. Has Cassie's first tooth come through yet?'

After blowing her nose, Lyn followed Della's lead and filled her in on news of her offspring.

Della laughed as Lyn reached the end of an anecdote. 'You should write all this down. You'd fill a book in no time, and I bet lots of parents would relate to it.'

Lyn flapped a hand. 'I'm no writer. You and Luke were the ones with the monopoly on that. Or do I mean duopoly? See? I'm no good with words. And, speaking of Luke, what do you think of him moving back here?'

'Well…' She scratched her cheek thoughtfully. 'I find it hard to believe. I can't imagine him finding life here exciting enough, can you? I can't help wondering whether he's only come back to be near his family and friends while he gets over his divorce.'

Lyn frowned. 'You might have a point, but he won't talk about it. I think it would do him good if he did.'

'Perhaps he doesn't want to talk to you because you have a happy marriage.'

'I hadn't thought of that.' Lyn swirled the wine in her glass. 'You might be right. Why don't you see if you can get him to talk?'

Della nodded. 'I'm hoping that's why he wants to catch up tomorrow night.'

'Sure. Do your best. Of course, we might be wrong. He might have moved back because he's sick of the dangers and deprivations of living like he has for so long. Maybe he wants to settle down and live like a normal person.'

'Could be as simple as that.'

'Then again,' Lyn said, 'this is Luke we're talking about. He doesn't do settling down.'

Rushing through her front door the next day, Della cursed the senior consultants' meeting for going on so long. Now she wouldn't have time for the leisurely shower she'd planned to indulge in before Luke arrived. She started to remove her clothes on the way upstairs, finished the job in her bedroom and darted into the en-suite bathroom, where she took a shower in record time. She'd pulled on a pair of three-quarter length jeans and a short white T-shirt by the time the doorbell rang.

After finger-combing her hair on the way downstairs, she dragged open the front door. The meagre remains of her breath escaped when she saw Luke standing there. In his jeans, and a black muscle-skimming T-shirt, he looked young again. The embodiment of her fantasy. The man who'd come to her in her dreams night after lonely night, year after long year.

Her nerves buzzed with the thrill of being near him again, reminding her why she'd fallen for him in the first place. As she stared, a trickle of water ran down her neck, and with her nerves so taut it sent a shiver right through her.

'Hi,' she said.

He held up his hands. In one, he clutched a brown paper fast-food bag. In the other, a bottle of local wine. He turned it so she could see the label. 'Will this do? Should I have brought a white too?'

'It's fine. Go straight through.' She pointed to the end of the passageway. 'I don't think there's a rule about the right wine to have with burgers.'

'Great place,' he said, glancing into rooms as he went.

She followed him into the kitchen. 'Thanks.'

He began to unpack the bag on the central island. 'Seriously, I like this house. When was it built? Do you know its history?'

Della opened a drawer and retrieved a corkscrew. 'Well, since you ask—and you might be sorry you did—along with the others in the terrace it was built in the eighteen hundreds to entice Adelaide's wealthy residents down to the beach. Each house was rented out, furnished, for the princely sum of five pounds a week.'

'Really?' He grinned. 'Glasses?'

She reached into an overhead cupboard and took down two long-stemmed glasses. 'There are eight houses in the terrace, and would you believe they're the only three-storey Victorian houses on the seafront anywhere in Australia?'

He raised his eyebrows. 'I had no idea.'

'You can mock,' she said. 'But I think it's very interesting.'

'No, I'm not mocking. I love this type of history. Real lives. Do you know anything else about it?'

'Well,' she said. 'They were originally linked to the shore by wide timber steps so the ladies could parade down to the water without soiling their skirts.'

Luke grinned. 'Love it.'

Della smiled back and perched on a bar stool, relaxing for the first time that evening.

* * *

Luke pulled out the stool next to hers. Instinct had told him she'd relax if he asked about her home. She seemed tense around him, and he didn't like it. Tension had never been a problem before. Not that he could remember anyway. He could only remember enjoying her company, having fun, being good friends. The best.

Maybe it was simply the length of time he'd been away. He unpacked the burgers, pushed one towards her and glanced sideways. She looked younger tonight. Less sophisticated, but no less beautiful. Without make-up, her oval face was lightly tanned, and her dark eyes were still striking with their long dark lashes.

Deceptively fragile looking, she could be taken for a teenager in her casual clothes with wet hair, no make-up, no bra.

He averted his eyes, focusing on his food. He'd had to struggle to avoid staring as a teenager, but he'd always known that if he tried anything with her, made any sort of move, it would ruin their friendship. She wasn't the type of girl to laugh off a sexual encounter. He didn't want to lose her company, so he'd looked elsewhere for his hormone-driven fun and kept his relationship with Della strictly platonic. Besides, Lyn would have killed him if he'd overstepped the mark. She was fiercely protective of Della. He hadn't rocked the boat back then and he had no intention of doing anything so stupid now. Yvonne had cured him of thinking he could have a relationship with a woman that wasn't based on sex or friendship. Either, or. Not both. He chewed for a few moments, willing himself to concentrate on the food. He didn't want to think about Yvonne. This evening was all about recapturing the happiness of his youth. He missed it.

He cleared his throat. 'Waterfront properties must cost a bomb. How did you manage to buy this one on your own? Did you come into some money?'

She tilted her chin. 'No, I didn't come into money. I've worked for every cent. I saved hard.'

He heard the defensive tone in her voice and kicked himself for his insensitivity. *Good start.* He remembered how awed she'd been by his home in the early days. She'd liked nice things, and growing up poor had given her ambition. He remembered she'd sworn that, one day, she'd have nice things of her own. He'd known back then she had the determination to achieve whatever she set her mind to. And clearly she had.

He'd never seen the inside of her family home, but the outside had given him the general idea. Lyn had gone inside once and told him he wouldn't believe how bad it was.

He had Della to thank for opening his eyes to the fact that not everyone had his advantages. And for giving him some idea of the pride a person in her position could possess. When she hadn't been able to afford to go to the places he and Lyn had taken for granted, embarrassment had prevented her from letting them pay for her.

He'd witnessed her mortification when, being so much smaller than Lyn, she'd been offered his sister's outgrown clothes. She'd rather have mended her old ones than accept them. It had taken all of Dawn's and Lyn's ingenuity to find ways of giving her stuff without taking away her dignity. And from this he'd learned lessons which had served him well in later years, in other circumstances.

He glanced around the extended kitchen and family room. 'You've done well,' he said gently.

Her posture softened. 'To tell the truth, I got it relatively cheap. Seaside land wasn't valued as highly when I bought it three and a half years ago. People have wised up since then, and the beach lifestyle has taken off in a big way.'

'So you'd just bought it last time I came over? I don't remember you mentioning it.'

'You were very busy on that trip.'

He grimaced.

'Plus, it was more than run down. It hadn't been touched for fifty years, which was why no one else took an interest in it. But I would have been too embarrassed for you to see it as it was then.'

He scrunched up the burger wrapper and wiped his hands on the paper napkin. 'You renovated it all by yourself?'

She nodded. 'I think I've kept a strong sense of the past, though, don't you? It has the original wide Baltic-pine floor-boards, the old marble fireplaces, iron lace on the balconies.'

'You've done a great job.'

It was much more homely than the place he'd shared with his ex-wife. She hadn't had the home-making gene. He picked up his glass and strolled to the French doors facing the back garden. 'Oh,' he said.

Della swivelled on the stool. 'Don't look at the garden. I haven't been able to do anything about it yet.'

'Lack of time?' he said, turning his back on the less-than-inspiring view.

'Well, that and lack of money. When I—' She grimaced. 'I mean *if* I get the promotion Dawn mentioned the other night, there will be more money to spare. The garden is next on my list of priorities.'

He saw the glint of determination in her eyes before she lowered them, gathered their wrappers and slid off the stool.

'I heard about the death of your parents,' he said. 'I was going to send flowers or a card, but sympathy didn't seem...appropriate somehow.'

She nodded without looking up from the bin where she dumped their rubbish.

'So, I didn't. I hoped you'd know I was thinking about you.'

'The irony of it is,' Della said in a flat tone, 'after years of wishing they were dead, I'd finally forgiven them. I tried to show it by being nice to them and paying for a holiday. I don't know whether it was for their sake or for mine.' She shrugged. 'Maybe I was just trying to show them I had money. I don't know, but, in an effort to show I didn't want them dead any more, I sent them to their deaths.'

He gave a violent start. 'Jeez, Della. That's a bit dramatic. It was an accident, wasn't it?'

'Of course it was, but it's still true. They'd never been out of the state. Never been further than the Adelaide Hills. Because I could afford it, I wanted to pay for a holiday in Melbourne, and because they didn't trust air travel they insisted on driving there.'

'And crashed on the highway.'

She nodded.

'You don't blame yourself, surely?'

'They would have been happier if I'd left them alone. Not to mention still alive.'

He exhaled, and returned to the kitchen island and the wine bottle. After refilling their glasses, he carried them to the coffee table located centrally in the family room. 'Come and sit down, Shrimp.'

She shot him a quick glance. 'I'll put the coffee on.'

'Leave it. Just sit down. Drink your wine.'

She hesitated, then walked to the armchair furthest from him and sat. 'Bossy.'

'Yes, well, I want you to relax. *I* want to relax. It's been a long time since I had someone to talk to. Someone on the same wavelength.'

She leaned forward, a sympathetic look on her face. 'You can talk to me.'

'I know. That's why I'm here.'

She nodded.

He leaned back, crossing his legs at the ankles, and took a

mouthful of the smooth wine. 'This is a good drop.' He looked into his glass. 'I'll be able to learn about wine now I'm back. When we were at uni we'd drink anything going, wouldn't we?'

Della still had an expectant look on her face. 'Luke, was it very painful?'

'What?' He tensed.

'The end of your marriage.'

He took another gulp of wine. 'I don't want to talk about that.'

'But...' She frowned. 'Isn't that why you're here?'

'What? No.' He shook his head for emphasis. 'Quite the opposite. I'm trying to forget about it.'

'It might do you good to talk about it. To open up.'

He made an exasperated noise in his throat. 'Shrimp, you sound like my mother. I came here because you were always so easy to spend time with. No pressure. We used to spend hours talking about anything and everything. Putting the world right. Remember?'

'I remember.'

He stared at her as she took a drink. He remembered those hours in her company as some of the happiest of his life. He wanted to find that peace again. He wanted to go back. But...so much had happened since then.

'What do you want to talk about, then?'

He shrugged. 'I don't know. Nothing in particular. Real estate?'

'Real estate?' Her eyes widened.

'Where should I buy a house? What should I look for?'

'I'm no expert. All I can say is, don't buy a "handyman's delight" unless you're prepared to spend years and lots of heartache sorting it out.'

'I think I could go for that. I mean, you do end up with something solid. Something concrete. Forgive the pun.'

'You? Renovating? I can't see it.'

'Why not?'

'Well, you always wanted to fix what was wrong with the world, not mend broken hinges. There's a big difference.'

'True.' He swirled the wine around his glass. 'But maybe I got tired of trying to fix the unfixable.'

Della watched him study the wine and got the impression he was seeing something else entirely. Something that made his eyes go dull and his mouth droop. It seemed the life he'd led had taken its toll. She thought back over some of the stories he'd covered. How could witnessing such human disaster not take a toll?

'Tell me about it,' she said softly.

He looked up as if he'd forgotten she was there. A small smile twitched his lips. 'I don't think so.'

'You can. If you want to. It might make it easier to deal with.'

'I did nothing but talk about it all for years. I talked into my video camera and my web-cam. I talked and talked and nothing changed.' He shook his head, and she saw frustration in the hardening of his expression. 'What else could I do but talk?'

He fell silent, but his throat moved as if he was struggling to swallow. As if he was trying to force down rising emotions.

'I wondered why you gave it up, but I didn't like to ask in my emails. Did it all get too much?'

He lifted one shoulder in a half-hearted shrug. 'We seem to have drunk all the wine. Do you have any more, or shall I go out and buy some?'

'I have a bottle of Riesling in the fridge. Will that do?'

'Sure.'

She hesitated. She hadn't seen Luke so down. If he was looking for a way out of his despair, she didn't think alcohol was the way to go.

'Don't look at me like that, Shrimp. I'm not an alcoholic.' His face twisted suddenly. 'Oh, hell, I'm sorry.'

She knew exactly what he was apologising for. He didn't

need to spell it out. He and Lyn were the only people who'd known about her mother's problem. She used to be terrified she'd inherited the tendency, but so far she'd never felt the need to turn to drink. But, if she ever found herself in a loveless marriage as her mother had, who knew what would happen? Would she, like her mother, become a hollow shell— no room for any feeling but bitterness? Fists clenching at her sides as she remembered, Della gazed at Luke. 'It's okay. You weren't thinking.'

'I should have thought. Look, forget the wine. I've had enough anyway. Let's have that coffee you mentioned.'

Della stood, gathering their glasses and the empty bottle, and headed for the kitchen. After filling the machine with water, she scooped coffee into the filter and flicked the switch.

Turning away, she grabbed some mugs and placed them on the island, then leaned her elbows on the granite. He'd been watching her, and he smiled as she made eye contact.

'I hate seeing you like this,' she said.

'Then stop trying to get me to "talk".' He made quote marks in the air with his fingers. 'I don't need to talk. I need to forget. And you can help me do that.'

'How?'

'By being the same as you always were.'

She tilted her head. 'So you can tease me like you always did?'

He chuckled. 'Yeah. That's part of it.'

'What's the rest?'

'Just be you. Comfortable. Easy. Calm.'

She straightened and went to get the coffee pot. She could do that. She'd spent her life being calm for other people. If she could do it for Tom Dermont, she could definitely do it for Luke.

CHAPTER FOUR

AFTER they'd talked for hours, about all sorts of topics—current affairs, renovations, travel, food and more—Luke left Della's house and drove along the seafront for a kilometre or so, before pulling over. The only subjects they hadn't touched on were the ones he knew Della had wanted him to talk about.

Stepping out of the car, he crossed the road to stand above the beach. Lights blinked on a navigation beacon out at sea. Apart from muffled music from a house further along the esplanade, and the low, rhythmic sound of waves rolling in to shore, the night was quiet.

If he talked to anyone, it would be Della. But not yet. He wasn't ready to expose his emotions like that. Even to her.

He breathed in the fresh, cool, sea-flavoured air and shoved his hands in his pockets.

He liked being home, liked the peace of it. But he wasn't sure he'd done the right thing in coming back. In fact, he was almost certain he should go back to India. He was needed there. The children at the orphanage would be glad to see him.

There was still time; the job wasn't finalised yet. He could help them find someone else. He could go back.

He'd applied for the new job when he'd still thought he had a marriage. Yvonne would have been here with him. But

Yvonne wasn't the woman he'd thought she was. She'd let him down on all counts and his plans had come to nothing.

He should have pulled out then and kept his old job as Regional Director for the charity.

Except that something had told him it was time to come home. Something had drawn him back here.

He thought of Della. It was good to see her again. Really good. She'd always been a good friend. His best mate. Until now, he hadn't realised how much he'd missed her calming presence in his life. In his younger years, he'd always been on the move, always *doing,* always looking for the next adventure, the next thrill. Unless he'd had Della for company. Then he'd been happy to sit. Just to spend time with her. She'd soothed his soul.

He stood for a while, thinking, remembering. Life certainly hadn't been easy for her, and he hoped his own family had made up in some way for the 'neglect' she'd experienced at home. And neglect was putting a good spin on things— something she'd always done herself. It was ironic that she'd ended up as a spin doctor after all the practice she'd had with her family.

He pushed a hand through his hair. He hadn't been a great friend in recent years. He'd been far too caught up in his own life, his own problems, to spare much thought for how she was getting on. Not that she'd needed him. He wasn't conceited enough to think he'd been a big loss. But she'd been there for him when he'd needed a friend in the past, and she'd slipped back into the old role tonight without a word of complaint.

She deserved better from him than a careless slip of the tongue. He'd seen the flash of hurt in her dark eyes as he'd spoken and that was the last thing he wanted to cause. He needed to show her that he appreciated her friendship. As long as he was here, while he made up his mind whether he wanted to stay, he'd try to make up for being such a lousy friend.

* * *

Della flipped through the wad of media enquiries Bonnie had dropped on her desk. Now that the crisis had escalated, some of the messages had come from interstate reporters and she'd have to respond quickly or miss their deadlines. She was in the middle of one such call when Bonnie entered the office again, carrying the biggest basket of flowers Della had ever seen. She stared as Bonnie placed the basket on the bank of filing cabinets against the wall.

After mechanically finishing the call, Della hung up and looked at Bonnie. 'What's going on? Are you allergic to them?'

'Allergic to what?' Bonnie glanced at the arrangement. 'Gerberas?'

'Whatever.' She waggled a finger at it. 'Why have you brought those in here?'

'Duh, because they're for you,' Bonnie said.

Della rubbed her forehead. 'Why would I want the Reception flowers? Nobody will see them in here.'

'Silly. They're not the Reception flowers. They're for *you*. Here's the card.' She reached into the depths of the arrangement. 'Here.'

Della stared at the small white envelope, then slid her finger inside and ripped it open. Tom Dermont's way of saying thanks for all the work she'd done? Bit early to say thank you, though. They had a lot to do yet if his company was to come out of this crisis unscathed. Besides, it wasn't at all like him.

Opening the card, she read it three times before the words sank in.

Luke. An apology. As if he needed to apologise for anything.

She didn't need a bunch of flowers to know he hadn't meant to hurt her with his inadvertent alcoholic comment. She glanced up—not a *bunch*. More like half a shop. They were beautiful. She smiled at Bonnie who was still hovering in the doorway.

'A friend,' she said.

'Really?' Bonnie raised her eyebrows. 'I hoped it was a secret admirer.' She looked at the flowers again. 'I'll have to find a friend like that. Oh well, back to work.'

When Bonnie had gone, Della turned back to the card. He wanted to take her to dinner. Tonight. She leaned back in her chair and looked at the arrangement again. It was perfect for her hall table, and would co-ordinate beautifully with her colour scheme. A deliberate choice, she guessed, knowing Luke. Not that he'd appreciate her drawing attention to his sensitive side. But, there was no doubt about it, he'd make a wonderful husband.

She frowned. As much as she hated to think about it, she had no doubt he would have been a wonderful husband to Yvonne, yet his marriage had broken up. Why?

Despite her expectation, he hadn't wanted to talk last night. Oh, he'd talked all right. They both had. For a long time, and it had been great. Just like old times. Except, in those days, he hadn't had that haunted look in his eyes.

She chewed her lip. Something was eating at him. She knew him a sight better than most people—possibly better than anyone else did—and she was certain she wasn't getting the whole truth from him. She also knew that if she'd pushed and prodded all night long he wouldn't have opened up.

If he was going to talk, it would be in his own time. All she could do was be patient. Be there when he was ready. When he needed her.

It would be hard to hear; she knew that. It had been hell to meet the stunning Yvonne and feign happiness for the newly married couple. Pain had zipped through her whenever she'd glanced across the room at them, their heads together, giving each other private smiles.

What if they'd argued over having a family? Or, worse, he'd left Yvonne because she couldn't have children?

The irony of providing a sympathetic ear in those circumstances was just too cruel to contemplate. But she was getting ahead of herself. There was no point in worrying about something that might not come to pass.

That evening, not sure what to wear since she didn't know where they were going, Della opted for a simple coral-pink dress, knee-length, with spaghetti-thin straps. Hoping it wouldn't look out of place at either end of the restaurant scale, she applied her make-up carefully and topped off her outfit with some dangly bead earrings and her favourite perfume.

The doorbell rang as she slipped on some high-heeled sandals. Picking up her handbag, she headed down to the front door.

Her heart lurched and it took her a moment to find her breath.

Luke in a dark blue suit.

And a white shirt.

And a tie.

He looked better every time she saw him.

She swallowed. 'Wow.'

'Wow, yourself. You look beautiful.' He grinned. 'Like a shrimp cocktail.'

'Thank you, I think. But will I do? I mean, I didn't expect you to dress up.'

'You're perfect.'

Her heart gave an extra-hard thud. She had to remind herself he was talking about her clothes.

'Shall we go?'

She nodded, and after locking the door took the arm he offered and walked with him to the Saab. He opened the door and she hopped into the passenger seat. No need to be nervous, she told herself as she waited for him to walk around the car. Two friends going out for a meal. Nothing more.

And she was right. No need to be nervous at all. Luke treated her to a lovely meal. They talked like they'd never been apart, perfectly relaxed with each other.

The conversation approached a more personal level when he told her about some of the places he'd visited in his work as a correspondent. With a studied vagueness, he described a few atrocities which made her squirm. But he interspersed these stories with others that made her laugh so much, she had to use her napkin to dab at her eyes.

'You'll have to stop,' she said at the end of one. 'You're ruining my make-up.'

He smiled, and his tanned face creased around his sparkling silver eyes. 'It's good to hear you laugh, Shrimp. You always were my favourite audience.'

'Oh?'

'I never had to explain my jokes to you.' He refilled her glass. 'You got them.'

'So did Lyn.'

'Mmm. But she's my sister. She always felt obliged to tell me I was an idiot after she'd finished laughing.'

'Well…'

He held up a hand in a traffic-stopping gesture. 'Uh-oh. At least leave me the illusion you didn't agree with her.'

She smirked and sipped her wine. 'Do you really think you can settle back here?'

He hesitated. 'I thought I could, but…'

'But you'll miss all the excitement, won't you?'

'Excitement.' He leaned back, cradling his glass between two hands. After a long moment, a sigh lifted his shoulders. 'I got the need for excitement out of my system years ago.'

'Then, what's the problem? Why are you in two minds?'

'I'll miss the children. I do already.'

'The children at the orphanage?'

He nodded. 'All of them, but especially one. She was my little shadow. Her name's Sharma.'

Della tilted her head as she looked at him, his eyes half hidden by lowered lids. She thought she might be falling for him all over again. Every hour she spent with him made her feelings stronger. How would she cope if he decided to go back?

She gave herself a mental shake. She'd cope. Same as she always had. Still, it would be a good idea to protect herself at least a little. To guard against falling deeper in love with him. Allowing herself to need him would only be asking for trouble.

'When do you think you'll make up your mind?'

'Soon. It'll have to be soon.'

She nodded then, after looking at him for a moment longer, said, 'Luke… Tell me how you came to be working at the orphanage. I mean, one day you were travelling all over the place, doing your news reports, and the next you were running an orphanage. You never told us why or how.'

He looked up and for an instant she expected a flip remark, a casual deflection of the subject in his usual manner, but he closed his mouth and dropped his gaze again. 'I went to Bhopal to do a follow-up story. Twenty years on, and thousands still suffering—you know the type of thing.'

She nodded.

'And I assume you know what happened there?'

'Of course. It's a well-used example of how not to handle a public relations crisis.'

He huffed out a breath. 'Yeah, right.'

'The extent of the disaster is beyond comprehension.'

'Of the original incident, yes. But the effects continue to this day, and that's what people don't know. Children are still being orphaned at an alarming rate, their parents dying as a result of being exposed to gas twenty years ago. These children are taken to a charity-run orphanage eight kilometres from the town. I went there as part of the research for my story.'

He paused to ask if she wanted coffee. Della agreed, and they placed their order.

Sighing, he narrowed his eyes and continued. 'It was the first time I'd been to an orphanage.'

'It was difficult?'

'Yes and no. I spent most of my time playing cricket with the older boys.' He shrugged. 'But it was difficult to leave.'

'I'm sure the children appreciated your visit.'

He laughed. 'Believe me, I got more out of it than they did. I think I would have stayed then, if I could, but I had to move on to another story. There was always another story.' He sounded weary. 'Always another tragedy.'

'But you went back?'

'I found out that the charity ran orphanages all over Asia. I started to drop in on different ones when I was in the vicinity. God, it really opened my eyes to the scale of the problem.'

His eyes stared off into the distance, were still bleak when he looked back at her. 'Can you believe a hundred homeless children a day are picked up at the interstate railway station in Calcutta?'

She blinked, unable to imagine such a thing. 'That many?'

He nodded.

'That's...' She shook her head. 'But where do they all go?'

'To the orphanages in and around the city. Ours is one of several located on the outskirts of Calcutta.'

'I don't know what to say.'

'Nor me.' He lifted his hands, then let them fall to the table top. 'That was my problem. I'd been talking about all these tragedies I'd witnessed, but nothing I said ever made a difference. In the beginning, I set out to change things, but I couldn't. I just didn't know what to say any more.'

Della looked at his hands, lying motionless. On an impulse she reached out and covered both of his with her own. She rubbed her thumbs across the weathered skin of hands. 'You must know, Luke, that your stories did make a difference. If only a few people were motivated to donate to charity, or volunteer with aid organisations, or even just think about what was happening, it was worth it.'

He stared at their hands for a long moment then turned his over and captured hers in a warm grip. 'I didn't mean to whine on like this. Why don't you tell me about your plans for the garden?'

'Which garden?'

'Yours. You said it's next on your list of priorities.'

She frowned. 'You don't have to change the subject. You weren't whining. And, even if you were, I wouldn't mind. You're entitled to. Especially to me.'

She saw the muscles working in his throat as he swallowed. 'Are you going to design it yourself or get a landscaper in?'

She could see he had no intention of going back to a subject that clearly caused him pain. She thought about his question. 'I don't need a designer. I know what I want.'

'Tell me.'

'Hmm, you might regret this.' In detail, she described her ideal garden, right down to the exact plants, unable to keep the wistfulness from her voice. Hopefully, she wouldn't have to wait much longer. The next board meeting, only a month away, was the one where a decision would be made regarding the new partner.

The firm looked set to merge with another PR consultancy in the near future. The expanded capacity and global spread of the resulting company would increase potential earnings for all employees but, as a partner, she'd be well on the way to financial security for life.

When she finished her description, she grimaced. 'You must be bored to death.'

'No. It sounds good.'

'You don't have to pretend to be interested.'

He grinned. 'What are your plans for the weekend?'

'I don't have plans, I have work.'

'Working again?'

Della laughed. 'And you're strictly a nine-to-five person, of course.'

'You've got me there,' he said with a grimace. 'But you have to make time to relax, you know. Have some fun. Even I know that. It's important.'

'Don't you worry about me,' she said, jabbing a finger towards him. 'I'm fine, and I'll be working at home, so I'll have a break from the office.'

On Saturday, Della had been working for a few hours and had achieved more than she'd anticipated when she heard the doorbell. Without the distractions of the office—phone calls, meetings, colleagues dropping in for a quick brainstorm—she always managed to do more hands-on work. Today she'd finished proof-reading a brochure for an important new client, which meant printing could proceed on Monday.

She was considering her next task when she reached the door and opened it to find Luke standing on the step. She blinked at him. 'What are you doing here?'

'It's lunch time,' he said, holding up a plastic supermarket bag.

'Is it? Already?'

'Yes, and my bet is you weren't planning to stop.'

'Well…'

'No, just as I thought. What did I tell you about making time to relax?'

Rolling her eyes, she moved aside for him to enter, but he didn't move.

'Grab your door key. We're eating on the beach.'

She hesitated.

'What are you waiting for? You live right on one of the best beaches in the world. And do you ever use it?'

'Yes. Of course I do. Sometimes. Occasionally.' She sighed. 'Okay.' Picking up her keys from the ceramic bowl on the hall table, she also grabbed her mobile phone and clicked it onto the belt loop of her shorts.

'Do you really need that?'

'Yes, I do,' she said firmly.

He shrugged. 'Fair enough. Shall we walk for a while before eating? I bet you've been sitting all morning.'

'A stroll would be good.'

They headed north, away from the jetty and towards the sea. Walking became easier on the firm, damp sand near the water's edge. Glancing at a family playing beach cricket, Della felt a pang, and unhappy thoughts rushed into her head. She banished them, deliberately clearing her mind of everything but the beauty of the day. And walking. With Luke.

Glad she hadn't worn shoes, she relished the sensation of cool sand squishing between her toes. She loved this time of year. Spring. Warm enough to make the outdoors a real pleasure, but not too hot to move as it would be in a couple of months' time.

Luke glanced at Della by his side. She looked tired. 'Do you work every weekend?' he asked as they crossed a stretch of soft sand to sit in the shelter of large rocks, a man-made cliff to protect the fragile dunes from erosion.

'Most,' she said.

She flopped onto the sand, tucking her legs beneath her. Her shorts rode up as she did so, and he froze, staring at her smooth, shapely thighs, wanting to slide his hands—

He gave himself a mental slap. What was wrong with him? He'd controlled himself through the raging hormone years and he could do it now. A grown man should have more self-control.

True, she was a grown woman too. Not the girl who'd made him feel protective.

Was that the difference?

Whatever. He clamped down on his reaction to her body. He didn't want to horrify her by giving any indication of where his thoughts had just gone. He knelt next to her and opened the plastic bag.

'Baguette?' he asked, taking two long rolls from the bag.

'Lovely.' She accepted one and peeled back the cling wrapping. 'Did you bring something to drink? I'm kind of thirsty after the walk.'

'Flavoured mineral water.' He handed her a bottle and watched her balance the roll on her knees while she opened the cap and took a drink. She checked the mobile phone for messages before picking up the baguette and biting into it.

'So, what do you like about your job, Shrimp?'

'Everything,' she said, with a mouthful of bread and salad.

He tilted his head and studied her profile as she chewed. 'More specific?'

She turned back to face him. Mixed emotions flickered across her face, and he wanted to know what she was thinking. After several moments, she shrugged. 'I like the satisfaction of knowing I've done a good job.'

'Uh-huh. You could say the same about any job.'

She tore a bite from the baguette, chewed and swallowed. After a swig of mineral water, she narrowed her eyes at him. 'I like the challenge of finding the right communications solution for each situation, tailoring a programme to suit specific demands, knowing I helped the client to get his or her message across in the most effective way possible.'

He nodded. 'What about your clients?'

'What about them?'

'Do you like them?'

She hesitated. 'Most of them. There are bound to be personality clashes from time to time, but I'm a professional. I can deal with it. I pride myself on dealing with it. I just concentrate on doing the best job I can.'

A bright red frisbee landed on the sand between them, followed closely by a large, hairy black dog. Luke made a grab for the bag of food while Della picked up the frisbee. As she went to throw it, the dog jumped on her, paws on her shoulders, knocking her flat on her back.

'Hey!' Luke grabbed the dog by the collar and hauled it off. He looked down at Della, shaking on the ground, and anxiety knotted his stomach. While he was distracted, the dog twisted out of his hand and galloped along the beach, frisbee in mouth.

Luke squinted as his gaze followed the dog. He saw a small boy waving a leash in the air and shouting words he couldn't make out.

He bit down on the aggressive words he'd been about to yell. He couldn't be angry with a child. Turning back to Della, he dropped to his knees and wiped sand from her wet cheeks as gently as he could with his big, clumsy fingers.

'It's okay, Shrimp,' he said. 'He's gone.'

She opened her eyes, sand clinging to her damp lashes, and grinned at him.

She was laughing. Not crying.

He sat back on his heels. His muscles relaxed as the sudden tension that had gripped him eased off. He shook his head. 'I thought he'd hurt you. Or frightened you.' And he'd never felt so protective. Even more than when she'd been a vulnerable girl.

'Don't be a doofus,' she said, slapping his shoulder. 'He only wanted his frisbee.'

In a flash of memory he saw Yvonne, raging and demanding revenge on a little girl who'd spilled milk on her new shoes. His jaw clenched. He should have known then that their marriage was doomed. Yvonne would have wanted the black dog put down.

Love did that to you. It wrecked your decision-making ability. It made you marry someone you wouldn't even like under normal circumstances. It set you up to be hurt when a person showed their true colours. It gave them the power to break your heart.

Della scrambled to her feet and he snapped back to reality, moving quickly to assist her. Holding her arms, being so close, his nostrils picked up the faint scent drifting from her sun-warmed skin. It tickled his memory. 'God, you smell good,' he said before he could stop himself.

'I'm not...wearing perfume.' She looked up, her eyes wide. 'Oh, it must be my bath oil. Lavender.' She looked relieved.

'I guess it must be. I remember that smell.' It burrowed right down inside, reminding him of a carefree time and the sheer joy of being with her.

She shook sand from her clothes and hair. 'What else did you bring to eat? I'm still hungry, and my baguette is covered in sand.'

'There's cake or fruit. Take your pick.'

'Both. Fruit first then cake, please.'

She settled on the ground again and smiled at him. He felt a wave of warmth, filling him and surrounding him, and thoughts of Yvonne vanished.

'Well, thanks for lunch,' Della said as she unlocked her front door. 'I really do have more work to finish, so...'

'So you don't want to invite me in. I understand.'

She felt the warmth of his smile all the way to the soles of her feet.

'What about this evening?' he said. 'Shall we go out for dinner?'

'Again?'

'You have to eat.'

'I do eat. Actually, I can't go out with you tonight. I have other plans.' She felt a stab of guilt. She'd intended to be there for him whenever he needed her.

'I can't talk you into changing your plans and going out with me?' He reached out, brushing a little sand from her cheek with his knuckles.

Her knees nearly buckled at his gentle touch. 'I'm going to Lyn's house.'

Grinning, he stepped back. 'I'll catch up with you there, then.'

He walked off towards his car which he'd parked some way along the esplanade. He stopped to drop their lunch remains in a bin and turned to wave.

She waved back, before entering the house. It had been a long time since she'd enjoyed a lunch break so much. She hoped she would see him at Lyn's house. She was missing him already.

CHAPTER FIVE

DELLA'S plans with Lyn for Saturday evening involved a zillion paint-colour chips and a dozen fabric samples. Sitting in the middle of Jamie's bedroom floor, Della allowed him to use her as a hill-climb course for his cars while she sorted through the paint chips and handed a selection to Lyn.

'Try these,' she said.

Lyn held a fabric sample next to the window with the paint chips fanned out against the wall. 'I'm not sure about the cornice colour—' The doorbell rang. 'Bugger. We'll never be finished at this rate.' She plonked the bits and pieces on a chest of drawers, muttering under her breath.

'It's probably Luke. He said he might pop round while I was here,' Della said casually, despite her stomach muscles tightening the instant she'd heard the doorbell.

'Oh, that's all right, then,' Lyn said as she left the room.

Annoyed that she was so excited to see him, Della distracted herself by tickling Jamie. He giggled and tried to run away but she caught him, scattering cars across the floor. She was on her hands and knees gathering them into the centre of the room when the door opened.

'Watch your step,' Lyn said. 'Della and Jamie are playing with cars.'

Della looked up. Luke stood in the doorway, one shoulder leaning on the doorframe, a grin on his face.

'Not satisfied with the Mercedes?' he asked. 'Trying to take the boy's cars too?'

'I'll have you know I'm Mount Panorama,' she said in a mock huff.

'Aha! Australia's toughest race track. I believe you have a wind problem, though.'

She grimaced. 'Oh, shut up.'

Lyn shook her head. 'No idea what you two are talking about. But since you're here, Luke, make yourself useful and hold this fabric.' She flapped a hand as he moved towards her. 'Better yet, take Jamie into the other room and occupy him so Della and I can get this over and done with.'

Nearly an hour later, Lyn had finally settled on colour schemes for both children's rooms, and Della entered the lounge to see Luke sitting on the sofa, Cassie asleep on his lap and Jamie cuddled into his side, watching the cartoon channel.

Della's heart squeezed at the sight.

He looked up. 'I wish they'd had all these channels when we were kids.'

'Oh, come on,' Lyn scoffed as she came into the room behind Della. 'You didn't sit still long enough to watch television.'

He grinned. 'You might be right there.'

'I know I'm right. And you didn't grow out of your fidgets either, which is why I can't believe you're serious about settling down here.'

'Everyone has to settle down some time,' he said. 'And I might decide it's time.'

Lyn jammed her hands on her hips. 'Might? You haven't decided yet, then? I thought you were here because you had decided.'

With a rueful smile he said, 'I might pull out of the job and go back to India.'

'Mum will be devastated if you do. You shouldn't have told her it was definite.'

He flinched. 'I suppose not. In my defence, I wasn't thinking straight.'

'And you are now?'

He shrugged.

'So, talk to us about what's bothering you.'

'Give me a break, Lynnie. Women talk when they're under stress. Men do the opposite. By the way, I brought some wine. It's in the fridge.'

'Hmm. I'll get it. You sit down,' she said, pushing Della towards the sofa.

'I'm okay,' Della said. 'I'll give you a hand in the kitchen.'

'Sit!'

Della sat. 'Jeez, you're as bad as each other for bossing people about.'

'Sorry,' Lyn said in a softer voice. 'It's just that you never seem to stop working. You have to learn to relax.'

'I know how to relax.' She watched Lyn leave the room, then gave Luke a sideways glance. 'She's right. Dawn will be devastated if you leave now, but you shouldn't let that stop you if you really think you've made a mistake.'

He blew out a noisy breath. 'I don't know what I think. It feels right to be home, but...'

They sat in comfortable silence for a few minutes, then Lyn returned with three glasses of wine and a plate of crackers and cheese on a tray.

'So, Dell,' she said. 'Have you found a dress for next Saturday?'

Della rolled her eyes. 'No. I haven't even looked for one yet.'

'What are you thinking? You have people to impress if you're going to get this promotion.'

'I hardly think my dress will make the difference.'

'You never know. Is it worth taking a chance on? You should go to the little shop on Unley Road where I found my outfit for Patrick's birthday party. Remember the one? I bet you'll find something there for sure.'

Della nodded. 'I'll make time on Monday.'

'What's this dress for?' Luke asked, helping himself to crackers now Lyn had relieved him of the sleeping baby.

'It's a work function. Not going to offer fashion tips, are you?' Della said.

'Maybe. I could come to the shop with you. Help you choose. What are friends for?'

'No! As if I'd believe you. You'd let me go out looking ridiculous.'

'No, I wouldn't. You could never look ridiculous.'

She stared. Why wasn't he teasing her?

'And what about a date?' Lyn went on. 'You'll need an impressive guy or the dress will be wasted.'

'I'm planning to ask Michael.' Della rolled her eyes again. 'I know I've left it a bit late.'

'Will he be able to make it at such short notice?'

'Hopefully not.'

'I can make it,' Luke said. 'Next Saturday, you said? I'd be happy to help out if this Michael isn't available.' He looked at her over his glass as he took a drink. 'So who is he, anyway?'

Lyn laughed. 'He's Della's dentist. Such a romantic story. He asked her out while he had his hands in her mouth.'

Luke gave Della a long look. 'I didn't know. How long have you been going out with him?'

'I'm not going out with him.' She shook her head at Lyn. 'And don't start,' she warned.

Lyn laughed again. 'Oh, I'm sorry, but he's so weird.'

'He's not weird in general. He just likes my teeth.'

Luke's eyebrows shot up.

'No, I'm not going to tell you,' Lyn said, wagging a finger at her brother. 'You can use your imagination. I'm sure it's good enough. But honestly, Dell, I don't know why you attract these weirdos.'

'You go out with a lot of weirdos, do you?' He winked at her.

'Like Lyn said, I seem to attract them.' She took a cracker from the plate and bit into it.

Luke laughed. 'Well, I meant the offer. I'll go with you if you like. Or am I not impressive enough?'

She looked up. Not impressive enough? As if. 'No, you'll do. If you're sure you don't mind?'

'I don't mind at all.' Glancing at his watch, he got to his feet. 'I'd better go. I'm meeting someone for a late drink.'

'Ooh, anyone we know?' Lyn asked.

'No. It's about the job.' He looked down at Della. 'How do I need to dress on Saturday?'

'You'll need a tux.'

As she said it, the thought of him in formal attire made her insides bubble. Her hand jerked, and she quickly wiped a splash of wine from her jeans. Looking up, she found Luke watching her with a knowing smile. But he couldn't know. He couldn't possibly know what she'd been thinking.

'I'll text you the details and meet you there,' she said.

'No. I'll pick you up. If you have people to impress, we should do this properly.'

'Exactly,' Lyn chipped in. 'No need to tell anybody Luke's just an old friend. He's a suitable escort for a partner of the firm, isn't he? Tall, clean and not too ugly.'

'Thanks,' he said. 'And, don't forget, I don't have a disgusting tooth fetish.'

On Wednesday after work, Della found Luke waiting on her front doorstep.

'What are you doing here?'

'Thought I'd drop in and see the dress you bought for Saturday.'

Her eyebrows rose. 'Well, you're out of luck. It's being altered. One disadvantage of being so short—anything I buy is too long.'

'Right.' He didn't look disappointed.

'So, why are you really here?'

He grinned. 'Thought you might fancy a walk and a bite to eat.'

Della glanced down at her laptop bag and her bulging briefcase, then up at Luke's face. Damn, she was going to agree, and that meant she'd have to work through the night again. She sighed. 'You lead me astray, Luke Brayford. You always did.'

'On the contrary, I'm the one who made you relax when you were studying too hard. I'm good for you.'

She unlocked the door and pushed it open. 'Give me a few minutes to change.'

'Sure.'

As she ran up the stairs, she heard Luke walk through to the kitchen. Despite the disruption to her work schedule, she couldn't deny the thrill she'd felt when she'd seen him waiting there. It had seemed such a long time till Saturday.

She pulled on stretch white capri pants with a blue-and-white-striped T-shirt, then after a moment's hesitation she reached right to the back of her wardrobe and dragged out her old denim jacket, the same as Luke's. Lyn had one too, but she wouldn't be able to get into hers now.

She slipped her arms into the sleeves, and memories of the crazy day they'd bought the jackets came crashing into her consciousness—including the treasured memory of Luke carrying her from the ice rink after her heavy fall. She winced. It had been worth the pain to be held in his arms but she hadn't fallen on purpose. If she had engineered it, she'd have chosen a more glamorous bone to break than her coccyx.

Luke greeted her with a lop-sided grin. 'You still have yours too.'

'Uh-huh. Ready to go?'

He moved ahead of her to open the door. 'Remember when we bought them?'

'How could I forget the pain?'

She walked past him then turned to say something else—but the words flew out of her head when he lifted his eyes quickly with a guilty smile. Had he been checking out her butt?

He closed the door and joined her, taking her hand as if it was the most natural thing in the world. She didn't pull away. It felt good.

'Shall we walk on the beach or the road?'

'Beach,' she said.

A little while later, they climbed the broad steps from the beach into Henley Square, and after only minimal discussion headed for the restaurant on the south side of the square, one of Della's favourite places to eat.

Once they were settled and had ordered, she gave Luke a penetrating look. 'Did you come by tonight for a reason? You seem like you want to say something. Do you have some news?'

'News? You mean, whether I've decided to stay?'

She nodded, suddenly unable to speak past the lump in her throat. He'd been back such a short time and already she'd got used to him being around. His presence showed her how empty her life had been before.

He made a dismissive gesture. 'That's still up in the air, but you're right. There is something I need to say. I've been thinking, and I want to apologise.'

She allowed a long shuddering sigh to escape from her body.

She felt as if she'd been holding her breath for hours. 'Luke, what could you possibly think you need to apologise for?'

'The other night—you were trying to be a friend and I was abrupt. I didn't even thank you for trying.'

She frowned. 'What are you talking about?'

'I know I haven't been a good friend over the years. The occasional email can hardly be described as keeping in touch, can it?' He grimaced. 'I don't deserve you.'

'Rubbish.'

'No, it's true, and I want you to know that I do appreciate you. I always have. In those early years, your emails kept me sane.'

'Oh, Luke, they were nothing special.' She'd made sure they were nothing special. She'd been careful to keep the contents within the bounds of platonic friendship. And she'd stopped sending them altogether once he'd married.

'They gave me a link to normality. They helped me remember what life could be like, because sometimes it felt like suffering was all there was in the world.'

His pain seemed to transmit itself directly to her. With her chest aching, she said, 'I'm sorry you had such a bad time. Why did you keep going for so long? Why didn't you come home sooner?'

He shrugged. 'Blind faith, maybe. It took a long time for me to realise how powerless I was, how insignificant.'

'You were *not* insignificant. You won awards for your stories. People sat up and took notice.'

He shook his head sadly. After staring out to sea for a long moment, he gave her a small smile. 'Once I'd filed my stories, I tried to forget about them. But they're all there, all filed away in the grey matter. And you know how the memory works… At the oddest times the most trivial event or a chance word can trigger a flashback and then I relive the whole experience.'

'That must be awful.'

He hesitated. 'It is. I can't tell you how awful. It's the children. In any disaster—earthquake, explosion, flood, war—it's the children who suffer most and who go on suffering, often without their parents or anyone to love them.'

He stopped abruptly and reached for her hand. Turning it over, he linked their fingers. 'Anyway, I wanted to say that I'm grateful you've always been there for me. I'm glad you're here now.'

Tears stung her eyes, and she struggled to keep them back as she squeezed his hand. 'If you want to talk some more...'

'You'll be the first to know.' He smiled. 'I like that there's no pressure with you, Shrimp.'

She smiled back. 'Me too.'

That Saturday night, Luke drummed his fingertips on the steering wheel while he tried to straighten out his thoughts. He'd arrived early, which gave him an opportunity to sit in the car. Thinking time. Not that he *could* think. The ability seemed to have deserted him.

The problem was, half the thoughts he'd been having lately were inappropriate ones. About Della. His best friend. And they made him feel like a traitor.

Since Wednesday, when she'd worn those white pants that had clung to her slender curves, and through which he'd seen the outline of her skimpy underwear, he'd kept imagining her *without* the pants. And he was terrified she'd guess when she looked into his eyes.

He pushed back his shirt sleeve to see his watch. His time was up. He had to go and knock on Della's door and hide what he was thinking. After one more deep breath, he climbed out of the Saab, telling himself he could do it. He'd mastered his urges years ago where she was concerned and he would do it again. He would look at her beautiful face and hear her sweet voice and remember that they were friends. Not lovers. They would never be lovers.

Still, the idea of her going to this dinner with anyone else had twisted his gut. He straightened his tie and walked to her front door. After a short delay, the door opened.

'Whoa!' He stared.

'Do you like it?' She gave a tentative twirl and the spectacular, bronze-coloured strapless number swirled around her calves. 'I found it at the shop Lyn recommended.'

'You shouldn't shop anywhere else.'

She smiled and he felt like he'd taken a punch to the solar plexus. He watched her move to the hall table to pick up her handbag, and swallowed hard. Okay, he'd thought she was beautiful in pants and T-shirt, but this... This was something else. A shudder ran through him and he pulled himself up.

Remembering what he had in his pocket, he stepped over the threshold. 'Nearly forgot,' he said, taking out a slim velvet box. 'I thought you might like to wear this.'

'For me?' She looked up at him with those deep, dark eyes, expertly made-up again and truly sexy. He could only nod.

He saw her hand tremble as she opened the box and he suddenly wished it was more.

When she didn't react, he said, 'Lyn assured me it would go with the dress.'

'Did Lyn choose it?' she asked softly, letting the fine chain slide over her fingers.

'No, I chose it. I thought it would suit you, but I asked Lyn for a second opinion.'

'You shouldn't have spent so much money.' She looked up at him, her eyes shining. 'Friends don't buy each other such expensive presents.'

He frowned. 'Lyn didn't see a problem with it.'

'Did you buy her a necklace too?'

'Well, no, but...' He didn't know what to say. He was confused. Had he done the wrong thing? He'd really wanted to buy her something nice, and he'd wanted to see this particular piece on her.

He gestured at it. 'Are you going to wear it?'

'Of course.' She took it from the box.

'Shall I fasten it for you?'

She nodded, handing it back to him.

He stood behind her, nostrils filling with a classy perfume, not her usual scent, and he fumbled with the dainty catch. After a moment, he succeeded in fastening it and looked over her head at her reflection. She touched the multiple thread-like gold chains hanging vertically from the main one. It was delicate but striking. Just like her.

'It's beautiful,' she said.

'So are you.'

She lifted her eyes to meet his in the mirror, and he felt his heart thump in his chest. As if it had been dormant and a shock had jolted it back to life.

'Thank you,' she whispered.

He cleared his throat. 'My pleasure,' he said. And he meant it. A seriously satisfying pleasure. He dropped a light kiss on the top of her head and moved away before he was tempted to do more.

Arriving at the convention centre, Luke drew Della's hand through his arm before they walked through the door. 'We have to do this properly, remember.'

Intercepting an admiring glance from one of the many young men in the foyer, he pulled her closer. He felt incredibly proud to have her on his arm. So much sex appeal in such a small, neat package. But he didn't want every other man at the function seeing what he saw or feeling what he felt.

'I must say, you scrubbed up surprisingly well, boss. Very sexy.'

Luke lifted his eyebrows at the slim arty type in front of them. Della introduced them and he shook hands briefly with her assistant, resisting the urge to teach him a lesson in manners. Della deserved more respect.

As the young man moved away, he said, 'Tell me, what is this function in aid of?'

'Sorry, I should have said. It's the firm's main client hospitality effort of the year, appreciation for their business, you know how it goes. Marvin—my boss—likes to splash out on this dinner, and it's become quite a popular event.'

'Poor Michael. His loss.'

She flashed him a mini glare. 'Let's leave Michael out of this. Now, I'd like to take a take a look at the seating plan. I didn't have a chance to see it at the office, and I want to know who's on our table. All the staff have to host one or two clients.'

'I can feel a migraine coming on,' he said with a grimace.

She gave him a sharp look. 'You've never suffered from migraines in your life. Listen…' She edged him around so they were out of earshot of the growing crowd. 'You won't start an argument tonight, will you?'

'With you?' he asked in surprise. 'I wouldn't. Not a serious one, anyway.'

'Not with me. With the clients. Just promise you won't. Please?'

How could he resist when she bit her lip like that? His gaze rested on the mistreated lower lip, and he felt an urge to kiss it better.

'Luke?'

He started. 'I promise. I intend to be the perfect escort.'

He led her to the freestanding notice board near the entrance to the main room, and while she studied the seating plan he took two glasses of champagne from a circulating waiter. As he sipped from one, he gazed around the foyer. It was filling up fast. Lots of impeccably dressed women, some of whom glanced his way, the message in their eyes unmistakeable. They could keep what they were offering. He had the most beautiful woman in the room at his side. Why would he be interested in any of them?

He froze with the glass halfway to his lips. What was he thinking? He wasn't interested in them because he'd just emerged from a wreck of a marriage that had destroyed the appeal of women and relationships. Not because of Della.

Just then, she muttered something unintelligible.

'Problem?' he asked, handing her one of the champagne flutes.

'Oh...' She gave a tiny shrug. 'Marvin's allocated us Tom Dermont, and to be honest I've seen more than enough of him over the last couple of weeks.'

'Ah.'

'His wife's okay. His production manager will be on our table too, and he's a nice guy. And then there's Melanie, their PR officer.'

'Anyone else?'

'Yes, Stefano, their sales manager.'

'And do we like him?'

Della smirked. '*I* do. You can make up your own mind.' She touched Luke's arm. 'It looks like people are going in to dinner.'

A couple of hours later, Della tried to catch the wine waiter's eye as he moved to fill up Tom Dermont's glass again. But the waiter didn't see her, and she couldn't risk making it obvious that she wanted to limit her guest's alcohol consumption.

According to the place cards, they were meant to be seated in the traditional male-female pattern but, as soon as Tom had arrived, he'd decided Luke would be a more interesting neighbour and had commanded his wife to swap seats. As a result, Tom had monopolised Luke all evening and she'd hardly had a moment to talk to him.

She shouldn't be jealous. She should be grateful she'd been spared the chore of keeping Tom entertained. She'd had the much more pleasant task of chatting to Dan Barlow on her right. She'd expected Dan to have a serious-minded partner, so Gina surprised her, but she seemed pleasant enough despite the nervous giggles.

'I mean, it stands to reason, doesn't it?'

Della cringed as Tom's voice boomed, clearly audible above the live music.

'You don't go to a brothel looking for a virgin, do you?'

She shot a glance at Gayle Dermont, Tom's wife. The poor woman plucked at his sleeve in a desperate bid to attract his attention.

'What is your problem?' he asked eventually, turning a glare on his wife. 'Can't you find anybody else to annoy?'

Della felt a surge of sympathy for Gayle, whose face turned bright red.

Tom turned back to Luke. 'What was I saying? Oh yeah, likewise, you don't buy a house next to an industrial zone if you want fresh air, do you?'

Della had to do something. Other guests were sending curious glances their way. She searched for a safe topic of conversation to introduce.

'Hope they all get some gross disease,' Tom slurred. 'Might shut the buggers up for a bit.'

That did it.

'Luke,' she said. 'Sorry to interrupt, but this is my favourite song.'

'I know,' he said, turning from Tom. 'And I was about to ask you to dance.'

'Love to. What about the rest of you?' She glanced around

the table. 'Come on, guys, we must be the last table to stand up.' She was pleased to see Dan and Gina take the hint.

Luke led her to the dance floor.

'Sorry about this,' she said as he swung her into his arms. 'I couldn't think of anything else to do. I was desperate.'

'Gee, thanks.'

'You know what I mean,' she said as he squeezed her a little closer.

'Well, I've been looking forward to this all evening.'

'You have?' She tried not to notice the way his thighs rubbed against hers as they moved. 'I suppose you haven't had many opportunities to dance in recent years?'

He raised his eyes to the ceiling. 'Yeah, that's why.'

A few moments later, Gayle Dermont tapped Della's shoulder. They paused at the edge of the dance floor while Gayle explained she'd persuaded Tom into a taxi. Della thanked her and watched her leave. Good thing too, she thought. Much more of Tom's tactlessness and she would have had to shut him up by inserting a fist into his mouth. Not a good move for someone in her position. But he could provoke a saint, and she'd never claimed to be one.

'Thank God for small mercies,' Luke said when Gayle had left. 'Now we can relax for what's left of the evening.'

'Mmm.' She wasn't so sure. Relax? How could she relax when she was crushed against Luke's body, feeling her carefully constructed defences crumbling?

Pity she'd chosen a slow song as her spur-of-the-moment favourite. Minutes earlier and they'd have been bopping around with floor space between them. Tom Dermont had lousy timing.

Luke's hands on her back seemed to caress her, even though they weren't moving. She was going crazy. Too much stress and not enough sleep. Still, she sent up silent thanks to the style gods who'd stopped her buying the silver dress with the deep dip at the back. Skin on skin would have been too much to handle.

'How much longer do we have to stay?' Luke murmured into her ear.

She started to pull away. 'We can go now if you like,' she said, stifling a spurt of disappointment.

'No.' He held her firmly in place. 'Not yet. This is too nice.'

She slid her hands back to his shoulders with a sigh. He wasn't wrong.

'But I'd rather not spend any more time at the table, watching Dan Barlow drool over you,' he said.

'What?' She glanced over her shoulder to where Dan and Gina were locked together in a very close dance. 'He's doing no such thing,' she scoffed. 'He has Gina.'

Luke chuckled. 'Trust me. A man knows when another man is interested. And I can tell you for a fact that Dan has one almighty crush on you.'

She ducked her head and stared at his tie. 'You're wrong. As if anyone would have a crush on me.'

He squeezed her close. 'Don't you know how gorgeous you are, Shrimp?'

His voice was scratchy. The music stopped. Della stood still. Blood rushed through her veins, pooling in her cheeks, making her hot. She needed air.

'Let's go,' she whispered, slipping out of Luke's arms and heading for their table.

She said her goodbyes and, as soon as Luke had done the same, made for the door. He followed closely behind, she knew without looking.

Luke made no move to touch her as they crossed the foyer. No fingertips on her back to guide her, no hand under her elbow. Which was fine by her. Her body was still humming from the dance, from having his arms wrapped around her, from being closer to him than she could ever remember.

When they stepped out of the lift, he moved ahead of her to open the car door. As she gathered the fabric of her dress into one hand, he touched her shoulder. A jolt like an electric shock shot through her, sparked by the unexpected contact.

'You really are beautiful,' he said. 'Don't you forget it.'

She looked up. He smiled and her heart restarted with a bump, sending hot blood rushing through her body.

He thought she was beautiful?

Luke, who'd always teased her, who'd seen her at her worst, thought she was beautiful?

Moistening her lips, she opened her mouth to speak but could think of no smart comeback. 'Okay,' she murmured before stepping into the car.

Okay? That was all she could manage? Pathetic. Della did a mental eye-roll as she arranged her dress so Luke could close the door. Leaning back against the leather seat, the new-car smell surrounding her, she dragged in a deep breath. But why had he said it? Did he think she needed an ego boost? Or...was he looking at her differently?

Resting her hands in her lap, she saw they were shaking and tucked them beneath her thighs. Her hands never shook. Wasn't she a crisis expert? Where was her famous compo-sure? Truth was, it had collapsed bit by bit from the moment Luke had arrived at her front door tonight.

He manoeuvred the car out of the multi-storey car park and across North Terrace without a word. They'd left the square mile of city and were heading to the coast before either spoke. Luke glanced across. 'All right, Shrimp?'

Della lifted her head from the seat back and nodded. Turning away, she stared out of the window at the lights of the suburbs flashing by.

You really are beautiful.

Could he really be seeing her in a different light? And, if he was, what would it do to their friendship? She couldn't let him spoil it. Not after she'd hidden her own feelings for so long to protect it.

He certainly wasn't over his marriage break-up. If he was thinking of her as a woman rather than a friend, it had to be some kind of reaction to the loss. A rebound affair. She couldn't...she simply couldn't allow that to happen.

She had to be strong.

Della's brain registered the black expanse of the ocean as the car rolled to a standstill. Before Luke had even taken the key from the ignition, she stepped out and was making for her front door as quickly as the cut of her ankle-length gown allowed.

'Della?' Luke called from the car. 'Wait.'

In the stark light of a street lamp, she dipped her hand into the little clutch bag, searching for her keys. How could they disappear? This wasn't her big, regular bag.

'What's the hurry?'

She looked up to see Luke standing tall and relaxed on her doorstep. 'No hurry,' she said.

Despite his casual tone, she could see a glinting intensity in his eyes. A trembling sensation filled the pit of her stomach. 'I just...I thought...you might...'

'Thought I might...?' He moved closer. 'Do this?' He touched his lips to the sensitive skin below her ear.

A squeak forced its way from her throat. 'Don't,' she said, annoyed at how weak the word sounded. Not the firm rebuttal she'd intended it to be.

'Why not?'

'Because...because friends don't do this.'

'Do they do this?' He placed a gentle kiss in the centre of her forehead as he took hold of her shoulders.

'No...well...' She should stop him. She had to stop him. She couldn't let him kiss her.

'Or this?' He slid one hand around the nape of her neck

and pulled her closer, before planting a kiss at the corner of her mouth.

Against her will, her eyes fluttered closed and her head dropped back.

His mouth closed over hers.

His lips were as warm and firm as she'd always imagined. His kiss was tender, gentle, slow, making her own lips quiver. His strong arms slid around her waist and up her back, pulling her against him, drawing her closer still while he caressed her mouth.

Her insides melted.

He pulled away slightly. 'God, I've wanted to kiss you all night. Ever since I saw you standing there like a bronze statue.' He jerked his head towards her front door.

Ha! That was nothing. She'd wanted to kiss him since she was fourteen years old. He'd started something now by lifting the lid on her bottled-up longing.

She searched his face. His expression changed. From pleased with himself to shaken.

'What?' she said, her eyes widening. 'What's wrong?' Her voice sounded like it hadn't been used for months.

He stared at her. She saw him swallow deeply. 'You are so beautiful. And my best friend. I think I'd better go.' He stepped back.

Cool sea air struck her face and slid over her shoulders. She shivered. Without Luke's warmth, she had no protection from the chilly breeze. From anything.

'You should go in,' he said, concern in his voice.

She nodded and reached out a hand to the door, then hesitated. 'Is everything...all right?'

'Fine.' He shoved his hands in his pockets. 'You?'

She nodded, but disappointment streaked through her. She swallowed and slipped inside, holding on to the edge of the door as she turned. 'Will you...call me, or something?'

He nodded. 'Sure. Sleep well and don't work too hard.'

She watched him stride to the car and closed the door only once he'd driven off. Leaning against it, she wondered if they'd wrecked something precious.

CHAPTER SIX

FROM her bed on Monday morning, Della watched choppy waves wink like diamonds in the morning sun. She was late waking, but for once work didn't feel like a priority. As she lay there looking at the sea, the memory of Saturday night filled her mind again.

So much for being strong. If she'd pushed Luke away, told him not to be stupid, laughed off the first, tentative touch of his lips, nothing would have happened.

If she'd shown him she had no interest in changing the parameters of their relationship, he wouldn't have persisted.

But she hadn't. She'd weakened at the vital moment and, instead of protecting their friendship, had demonstrated the depth of her longing. She'd revealed the raw emotion she'd carried round for as long as she'd known him.

If he hadn't stopped things spiralling out of control, would she? She doubted it.

But he had ended the kiss and that spoke volumes about what he thought of her. She was good enough to keep him company, to spend time with, to talk to. Good enough to be his friend, but not to tempt him to take the kiss further.

He must have felt an attraction for her, or he wouldn't have kissed her. But it must have been fleeting. A whim. And it had passed. She could only hope he hadn't guessed the extent of her own feelings.

With a groan, she rolled out of bed. It was time she dressed for work but, as she began her morning routine, the thoughts running through her head were anything but routine.

A short time later Della strode into the reception area of the firm's city-fringe office building. Turning automatically to Bonnie's desk, she was about to issue a cheery greeting when Bonnie pre-empted her.

'Where have you been?' she snapped.

'Why? Is someone looking for me?' Della double checked her watch. 'I'm only a few minutes late.'

'Is someone looking for you?' Bonnie said, her tone flat with disbelief. She shook her head. 'I know they say you're calm in a crisis, but this takes the cake.'

'What does?'

Bonnie rolled her eyes. 'Don't tell me you really don't know?'

'Look…' Della tried to keep the exasperation from her voice. 'You can safely assume I don't know what you're talking about. Now, *is* someone looking for me?'

Bonnie stiffened. 'Yes. And, if I were you, I'd get a move on.' She nodded in the direction of Marvin's office. 'The boss wants to see you, pronto.'

'Thank you.' Della hadn't meant to be curt with Bonnie but she was in no mood for game playing. And, despite the hours of unpaid overtime she put in, she couldn't help feeling a twinge of guilt at being late. Sad but true.

Crossing an open-plan section, she entered the sanctuary of her own office. She'd drop off her briefcase and collect a coffee on her way to Marvin's executive suite. Whatever had happened—and she anticipated something to do with Tom Dermont—it would be easier to take with a coffee.

Taking a pen and notepad from her top drawer, she allowed herself to hope it wasn't a crisis, and just Marvin looking for congratulations on the success of Saturday's function. Her internal phone buzzed and, seeing Marvin's extension number in the display, she pressed the speaker button.

'Good morning, Marvin. How are you?' she said in her normal even voice.

There was a moment's silence and instinct told Della her greeting hadn't gone down well.

'You're in, then,' he said, his voice gruffer than usual.

'Did you want to see me?'

'In my office.'

'Sure.' She reached for the button to end the call.

'Now!' he barked as though she hadn't understood.

'Of course. I'm on my way.'

Apprehension prickled Della's spine as she gave up the idea of grabbing a coffee and hustled out of her office. Whatever Marvin wanted, it didn't sound good.

She took a moment to peer into Jason's cubicle on her way and found it deserted. His computer was on so it seemed he, like Marvin, was in early this morning.

Straightening, she scanned the area over the top of the cubicle partitions. No sign of Jason, but she caught the eye of one of the other senior consultants, her main rival for the new partnership. As she lifted a hand in greeting, he turned away. Her hand dropping to her side, she spun on her heel and walked on.

Could it be Marvin had early news regarding the partnership? Had she got it? Had her appointment ruffled some feathers?

With a brief knock, she entered Marvin's office and her eyebrows rose in surprise at seeing Jason installed in one of two chairs facing the desk.

'There you are,' she said. 'I've been looking for you.'

Jason glanced her way but didn't make eye contact. Puzzled, she looked at her boss. He ran a finger around his shirt collar, but the action didn't lessen the heated flush of his face. Something had to be seriously wrong. Switching to efficiency mode, she took a seat. 'What is it, Marvin? I take it we have a problem?'

He stared at her. 'Either you're an incredible actress or you haven't seen this morning's newspaper.'

'I haven't.' She pictured the paper, still in its plastic wrapper, lying on the hall table where she'd left it. 'It's normally the first thing I do but I was running late. What have I missed?'

He hesitated, then handed her the South Australian daily, folded in half. The major headline of the day took up half the front page:

Dermont's Disdain:
Residents Don't Matter

'Oh my God.' She scanned the text of the article, seeing comment after comment attributed to Tom Dermont, and taking in a poignant photograph of a young child with a nasty skin rash.

'I don't understand,' she said. 'How did they get access to all of this stuff?' She turned the page and found more photos plus a whole bunch of damning data. This was no lightweight story.

'Surely Tom wouldn't give an interview like this? Why would he even talk to the press without involving us?'

'But he did involve us. We, or rather *you,* arranged the meeting.'

She looked up, startled by the accusation. 'I beg your pardon? I didn't do any such thing. Why would I?'

Marvin looked at Jason.

Della turned to her assistant. 'You? Did you do this?'

'No!' Jason gripped the arms of his chair.

'Jason simply filled me in,' Marvin said.

'Look at the by-line.' Jason nodded at the newspaper on her lap.

She closed the paper and ran her eyes over the front page, looking for the name.

She found it.

Her throat constricted.

Oh God.

Luke Brayford.

After a long moment of silence, Della looked up, meeting Marvin's glare. He slapped his desk with the palm of one hand, and she fought to stay calm.

'Did you or did you not take Luke Brayford with you on Saturday night and sit him next to Tom Dermont?'

'I did,' she said softly. 'But—'

'For God's sake, Della! Jason says you let him talk to Dermont all night without monitoring his questions.'

She flashed a glance at Jason, but she knew the annoyance she felt with him was only a fraction of the anger she'd feel for Luke when she allowed herself to think about what he'd done.

'He did talk to him, but it wasn't meant to be an interview...' She let her words trail off. They were worthless. How could she have trusted Luke with Tom Dermont? He might have left the job, but underneath he was still a journalist. She lifted her chin and waited for Marvin to speak.

'As you can imagine, I've already had Dermont on the phone,' he said. 'Demanding your dismissal.'

She wouldn't react to Marvin's words. Her grip on the newspaper tightened but she gave him a cool stare.

'Gross incompetence, he claims. And I have to agree with him, Della.'

So did she. But she didn't deserve to lose her job. Not after all the work she'd put in. Not after all the crises she'd handled with unrivalled success. This couldn't be happening.

Marvin sagged. 'You know I have to let you go. I'm devastated, Della. You've been a real asset to this firm.'

He was devastated? How did he think she felt—after all the effort she'd put into building a career, for this to happen now?

Marvin rubbed his chin and the scrape of it filled the silent office. Suddenly, he straightened. 'I have no choice. Clear out your desk and vacate the premises within…' He glanced at his watch. 'Thirty minutes. Your employment with this firm is terminated with immediate effect.'

Della swallowed her gasp. 'Don't you think you're being a little hasty? I could—'

He held up a hand. 'Don't make this more difficult than it has to be on either of us. We need the Dermont account, especially now, with the merger in the balance. How would we look if we let our biggest client go for the sake of one employee? I will not do anything to jeopardise the account, and Tom insists you have to go. Nothing less will satisfy him.'

He flicked open a folder on his desk. 'Now, I have a tremendous amount of work to do if I'm going to repair the damage you've done.'

She tossed the newspaper onto his desk and stood, smoothing down her straight skirt.

'I would have expected more support from you, Marvin, considering all I've done here.'

He grunted.

Burning bridges in business was never a good idea. Who knew when she might run into Marvin or Jason again in other circumstances? Either could be in a position to make or break her career in the future… If she had one. Turning, she walked from the office with all the dignity she could muster.

Determined to keep herself together, Della tossed her personal effects into a cardboard box as quickly as possible.

Nobody spoke when she walked through the open-plan office space, carrying her box. She was glad of it. Giving a brief nod to Bonnie as she crossed Reception, she forced herself not to run through the door. Only when she was in her car, doors locked, did she allow herself to think about what had happened.

Now she knew her worth to the company. Tom Dermont's money had spoken a hell of a lot louder than her contribution could. All of the effort, all the long hours, had been for nothing.

And as for Luke.

Pain speared her chest. How could he have done this to her?

Had he gone to the dinner with the intention of grilling Tom Dermont? Logic told her he couldn't have known they'd be seated together. But, even so, he'd taken advantage of the situation.

She should have realised he had an interest in the Dermont's plant. He'd made the effort to go to the press conference on only his second day back in the country. But she'd been conceited enough to think that had been for her sake.

Like an idiot, she'd handed Tom to him on a platter, and he'd gobbled him up and spat him out. Not that she cared about Tom. He deserved whatever he got. Especially after what he'd done to her today. But hadn't Luke given her a thought? Didn't he care what happened to her? Did he think Della losing her job was justifiable collateral damage as long as he got his story?

Tears welled in her eyes. Her forehead dropped against the steering wheel with a thud.

How could she have been so stupid?

He was supposed to be her friend, yet he'd used her position to expose her client. And, to cap off a successful evening for him, he'd kissed her.

She sat for a moment, letting the truth settle in her veins like iced water, then straightened, brushed the tears from her eyes and started the engine.

She didn't want to go home, to the house her job paid for—the job she no longer had—so she turned towards Lyn's.

Lyn opened the door to her with the newspaper in her hand and a puzzled look on her face.

'What are you doing here? Why aren't you at work?'

Della shook her head as she stepped by Lyn and went into the lounge. Feeling almost light-headed, she slumped into the sofa. 'Where are the children?'

'Jamie's at kindy and Cassie's asleep,' Lyn said as she sat in the chair next to the sofa. 'What's wrong?'

Della waved a hand at the newspaper on Lyn's lap. *'That's* what's wrong. Your brother's story.'

Lyn frowned down at the front page. 'I was just reading it when you rang the doorbell. From what I've read so far, it seems pretty good.'

'Oh, I'm sure it is. I'm sure he's done a thorough job,' she said sarcastically.

Lyn's head came up. 'But—'

'Why? Why did he do it?'

'I suppose he thought he should.'

With a groan, Della dropped her head into her hands.

'Dell, hon? I must be having a dumb day. Tell me what's wrong.'

'I've lost my job,' she wailed. She felt tears stinging her eyes but she was too nauseated by the whole situation to let them fall. 'They fired me over that,' she said, pointing a shaking finger at the newspaper.

'Oh, Dell, I don't believe it. Why would they do that?'

'Because I took Luke to the dinner and let him talk to Tom Dermont.'

Lyn stared. 'Well, that's just dumb. As if you could stop him. You can't control Luke's actions.'

'No, but I should have known better.' She sighed. 'I can understand Marvin. I don't like it, but I can understand why he did it.'

'I can't. All those hours you put in for that firm. All that work you did when you should have been relaxing. It's just... It's not on, Dell. They're totally in the wrong to sack you.'

After a moment, Della said, 'It's Luke I don't understand. I can't believe he did it.'

Lyn grimaced. 'Did what—cared enough to try to help people who can't stand up for themselves?'

Della opened her mouth to argue, but couldn't bring herself to tell Lyn she was off the mark.

'I'm truly sorry about your job, Dell, but you know my brother as well as I do. Well enough to know he considers it his duty to challenge injustice. Of course he wouldn't be able to stand by and ignore such blatant disregard for the health and well-being of ordinary people.'

Lyn paused but Della remained silent.

'And really, when it comes down to it, would you want him to change?'

Della jerked one shoulder.

'Well, I know I wouldn't. I've always been proud of my big brother and the way he makes a stand for what he believes in. Not many people have the courage to do what he does.'

'No.' Della dragged a sigh from deep down. 'Of course I wouldn't want him to change. But he used me, Lyn. He used me to get to Tom Dermont, and he didn't care about the consequences to me.'

'Well, firstly, I don't think he used you at all. I'm sure he didn't go to the dinner with the intention of grilling Tom Dermont. And, secondly, why would he have thought there'd be consequences to you?'

'He knew Tom Dermont was my client.'

'So? That doesn't mean he knew you'd get fired over your client choosing to talk to someone who then wrote a story on that client's plant. If anything, he probably thought your firm would get more work out of it. After all, Dermont needs good PR more than ever, doesn't he?'

Before Della could answer, the doorbell rang.

Lyn went to the window. 'It's Luke. Good, we can ask him—'

'No!' Della jumped to her feet. 'I don't want to see him. I can't, I'm too angry.'

'Oh, Dell…'

'No. I can't talk to him now. I have to go. I'll leave through the garage.' Running out of the room as she spoke, she saw Luke's tall silhouette through the front door and her heart thudded against her ribs. The last time she'd seen him she'd kissed him. Now she was running from him. She was so confused, but she couldn't stop to sort out her thoughts now.

Several minutes later, Luke stood at the window of Lyn's lounge, staring at the street. He could hardly believe what Lyn had told him. He would never have predicted that Della would lose her job over his story.

Would he have written it if he'd known?

Hard to say. He probably would have done, though he might have talked it over with Della first.

He sighed. It was too late now. The damage was done. He just hoped the damage to Dermont's was extensive, as much for Della's sake as for the residents'. It would serve him right for demanding her dismissal.

Luke couldn't help feeling pleased that Della didn't have to work for Dermont any more. Though she hadn't admitted it, she couldn't be happy in a job that had caused her to compromise her own ideals. In time she would find another job and maybe she might even thank him for providing the impetus for her to find something else. He hoped so

In the meantime, he reminded himself, she had no income, and since financial security meant a great deal to her he couldn't blame her for being so angry with him.

And then there was the kiss.

He turned as Lyn entered the room carrying two coffees. He took one from her, mumbled his thanks and sat down.

Della had been reluctant to let him kiss her and he'd gone ahead anyway. Not that he'd forced himself on her. God, his whole being revolted at the thought. But he'd definitely ignored her initial protest.

But he hadn't imagined her response. It had sent his senses spinning. It had given him a buzz like he hadn't known since Yvonne. Hell, if he was honest, he'd never known anything like it before. He and Yvonne had gone from the bar to his bed before he'd even known her name. There hadn't been time for slow, seductive kisses.

But Della was his friend, not a woman he'd picked up in a bar. He couldn't go around kissing his friends, no matter how sexy they were. Not that there was any other friend he'd consider kissing. She was the only one who'd ever tempted him.

'Deep in thought?' Lyn asked

He started. 'Yeah. Sorry.'

'Trying to think of some way to make it up to Della, I hope.'

'Do you think I can?'

Lyn shrugged. 'I have no idea, but I do know you have to try. She doesn't deserve this, Luke.'

'No, she doesn't. Do you think what I did was wrong, Lynnie?'

Lyn sipped her coffee, then shook her head. 'I don't. And, deep down, Della doesn't either. But she's hurt. She thinks you used her and I can see her point.'

His eyes widened. She thought he'd used her?

'She feels betrayed.'

His chest felt tight and his tongue stuck to the roof of his mouth. He never wanted to hurt her.

'You should have heard Dermont, Lynnie. He was boasting about what he gets away with out at the plant.'

Lyn raised her free hand. 'I believe you, Luke, but there's no need to explain to me. It's Della you need to tell. And I wish you luck, because at the moment she's in no mood to listen. In fact, I think you should leave her alone for a few days. Let her get over the shock of losing her job.'

He sighed. Lyn was right. And it would give him time to think of something to do, some gesture to show her he regretted what had happened.

CHAPTER SEVEN

DELLA spent the next few days phoning contacts and putting out feelers, but with no luck. On Friday, she had her first interview. It didn't go well. Not surprising, since the man in charge was one of Marvin's friends. From the glances he'd given his human resources officer, Della guessed the guy hadn't done his homework. If he had, she wouldn't have made it to the interview list.

She drove home in a daze. What was she going to do? The next mortgage payment was due soon, and she'd already broken into her savings to pay the car loan. Her rainy-day fund would soon dwindle at this rate, and, as she'd put most of her savings into superannuation, she couldn't access the money now.

She parked in the street behind her house, meaning to put the car away in the rear garage later, and made for the gate to her back garden. When she reached it, she froze. It stood ajar—only a little way, but it had always been too stiff to open without an effort, so this was no accident.

Hearing movement inside the garden, she bit her lip and pushed the gate further open.

Luke!

She gasped. Shirt off, surrounded by all sorts of stuff, he was leaning on a spade. From the look of his sweat-streaked muscles, he'd been using it too. As she strode forward, he looked up, breaking into a smile.

'You caught me.'

She stared. Difficult not to, when he looked like this—in old denim jeans which had settled low on his hips, his muscles all pumped and shiny. Enjoying the view was only natural. Very natural. A basic instinct. But she wanted to know what the hell he was doing, so with an effort she lifted her eyes to his face.

'Caught you…doing what, exactly?'

He gestured at the ground next to him. 'Levelling the terrace. This is the lower one.' He pointed over his shoulder. 'I've already done the top one. I wanted it to be a surprise. I suppose it was too much to hope you'd be out all day.'

Two sandstone terraces, joined by steps, and a low wall with lavender cascading over its edge. Wasn't that what she'd told him when she'd described her ideal garden? She glanced around the space. It seemed even smaller now it was crammed with masses of pots, all containing well-established plants. Looking back at him, she demanded, 'What's going on?'

He aimed the spade at the ground, and the rasp as it sliced through the sandy soil set her teeth on edge.

'I wanted to do something to apologise for losing you your job. You did say this was next on your list of priorities.' He leaned on the spade again. 'I'm guessing it slipped even further down the list now because of me and my actions.'

Excitement crept around the edges of all her other emotions. She was going to have a garden and, knowing Luke, it would be the garden of her dreams. He never did anything by halves.

He lifted the spade from the ground and sliced it into another spot.

'The story had to be told,' he said without looking at her. 'And I hope Dermont loses his licence to operate as a result.

But I want you to know that I truly didn't believe you'd lose your job over it. I thought, if it had any effect on you at all, it would be more work, not less.'

She hadn't seen him all week, and she'd had time to think about her reaction to what had happened. Although she was still angry at Luke for writing the article, she knew that he couldn't be held fully responsible for her losing her job.

She sighed. 'There's going to be a state government inquiry, you know.' She'd heard the news on the radio. With everything else she'd had to think about, it had hardly made a ding in her consciousness at the time, but it had sunk in. 'Look, I know Tom's a big idiot, but the plant's not that bad. Now people's jobs are in jeopardy. All the people who work at the Dermont plant could be out of work if the government decides to shut it down.'

'It *is* that bad,' he said. 'And it could be their lives in jeopardy, not just their jobs. I'm surprised you're still defending him now you don't have to. If you'd heard what I've heard...'

'You've only heard gossip, sour grapes—'

'No. Give me some credit for knowing how to write a story, Della. I spoke to former employees, people who left the company because they couldn't condone the culture of carelessness rife there.'

'There have been a few leaks—'

'Not a few. A lot. And becoming more substantial with each one.'

'But they're harmless chemicals.' She flapped a dismissive hand. 'The latest one was an exception. They don't normally cause fires.'

'The latest one was impossible to cover up because of the fire, but it was only one in a long line of toxic leaks. We're talking about chemicals which are some of the most dangerous in existence, with the potential to cause death, disease and birth defects.'

Della hesitated. He made it sound terrible, but Tom had assured them…

'You're exaggerating,' she said. 'You must be. The only toxic leaks have been so small they couldn't have done any damage.'

'According to Dermont? What he's doing there is criminal. Cost cutting.'

'All large companies have to control costs. Employees are never happy about it.'

'Control, yes. But when it comes to safety, short cuts are bad news.'

He used his hand to wipe his forehead and she caught a whiff of fresh masculine sweat mixed with the remains of his deodorant, and she didn't find it at all repulsive. She straightened as a shiver trickled down her spine. Her body craved what her mind said she couldn't have.

'Look,' she said, 'it's too hot today to stand here talking. Do you want to come inside for a cool drink?'

He grinned. 'Sure.'

As he turned to grab his T-shirt from where he'd left it on a pile of sandstone pavers, she clamped down on a surge of disappointment that all his male magnificence was about to be covered. She walked ahead of him into the kitchen.

Once they were seated at the table, one of them on each side, Della sipped her lemonade and looked at Luke over the top of the glass as he tipped back his head and drank. Even covered in dirt, he was the best-looking man she'd ever seen.

After a deep drink, he put the glass on the table and leaned back in the chair. Shoving his hands into his jeans pockets, he said, 'I take it you haven't actually read the story?'

'No.' She hadn't been able to bring herself to do it. At first she'd been too angry, but since… She couldn't say why, but she suspected it was fear that had kept her from opening the paper— Scared of the shame she might feel.

'Remember we were talking about Bhopal the other day?'

'Yes. What about it? You're surely not implying Dermont's is anything like that plant?'

He raised his eyebrows but said nothing.

She shook her head. 'I don't believe it. Not here.'

'From what I hear, Dermont's have neglected safety measures for some time. Gas-leak prevention systems are either malfunctioning, shut down or simply inadequate. Tom Dermont personally ordered refrigeration equipment used to cool chemical storage tanks to be shut down so they could utilise the energy elsewhere in the plant.'

'But...there are inspections, maintenance systems...'

'Mmm.' He hesitated. 'Maybe the state government inquiry will be enough to make Tom Dermont lift his game.'

He shrugged, and she knew he didn't believe it would make a difference to Tom. He drained his glass, then smiled. 'Anyway, today is not about him. It's about saying I'm sorry you lost your job. And I am. Truly.'

'I know you are.'

'I hope you also know that I didn't use you. I wouldn't do that. I would have had to go to the dinner with the express intention of getting information from Dermont and I swear, Della, I had no such intention.'

She nodded. 'I understand that now. I must have been in shock when I spoke to Lyn. I wasn't thinking straight.'

'I admit I'd taken an interest in what was happening out there before the dinner, but I promise it never even occurred to me that Tom Dermont would be on our table. And, even then, I wouldn't have taken advantage of the situation if Dermont hadn't shown his true colours. I didn't ask him a single question. I didn't need to. He volunteered all the statements I used.'

'But he didn't know he was talking on the record.'

He made an impatient gesture. 'There's no such thing as

off the record. Nor should there be when it comes to endangering people's health, their very lives.'

With a sigh, she said, 'Luke, I know you didn't expect the repercussions it had. Let's just leave it at that. It's my problem now. I have to deal with it.'

He was silent for a moment. 'Would it help if I rang your boss and explained that you had nothing to do with the story?'

'God, no.'

'What if I offered to write a positive story about another client?'

She looked up. 'Only if you'd write one about Dermont's.'

She saw the answer in his eyes before she'd finished speaking. 'Actually, I don't think even that would be enough. But it doesn't matter. I wouldn't go back there now, anyway.'

There was a silence which Luke eventually broke. 'You'll be able to get another job easily, though, won't you?'

'Not a chance.' She rubbed her pounding forehead. 'Adelaide might as well be a small town when it comes to this business. The best I can hope for is to pick up some freelance work. Whether it will be enough…'

'I'm sorry. I know how much that job meant to you, even if it wasn't really you, Shrimp.'

'What do you mean? I did a good job.'

'I'm sure you did. But you've been living a compromised existence.'

'Luke…'

She made an exasperated sound. She found it difficult to argue with him. Her parents might have written him off as just another spoilt rich kid, but she'd known better. Much better. It wasn't a case of being nice to the little people; Luke, with all his wealth and advantages, had a strong sense of social justice, a genuine desire to make a difference.

She'd been giving all this plenty of thought since Monday and, as Lyn had said, she wouldn't want him to change. If he did, he would no longer be the man she'd fallen in love with, that she valued as a friend.

And, if she was honest, had she been less concerned with safeguarding her income, she would have walked away from dealing with Tom Dermont and people like him.

Having to defend Tom, portray him as a good guy, had been soul-destroying at times. She could admit now that she'd done a great deal of her job on auto-pilot, not thinking deeply about it, scared that if she did allow herself to think she wouldn't like what she was doing, wouldn't like the person she saw in the mirror.

'I think you put your trust in a broken compass,' Luke said.

She sighed. Bit by bit, he was chipping away at the façade she'd built. She didn't need to hear any more. Not now. She was still too fragile. She needed a change of subject.

Waving her free hand towards the French doors and her view of the garden, she said, 'You didn't have to do this. It must have cost a fortune to buy all those plants and pavers and God knows what else.'

He shrugged. 'You know I can afford it. You're going to let me finish it, aren't you?'

She smiled for the first time she could remember since Saturday. 'Sure. And I expect you to do a damn good job.' She'd forgiven him, but he didn't need to know just how much.

'I will.'

She could tell from his narrowed eyes that he wanted to say something else, something that made him hesitate, unsure. Her stomach muscles tightened in panic. Was he going to bring up the kiss? She'd hoped they could forget it. It had been a stupid mistake. It should never have happened.

He frowned. 'Would you object to me making a suggestion?'

'What kind of suggestion?' she said warily.

'I know where you could pick up some freelance work.'

Her breath hitched. Panic subsided and she leaned forward eagerly. 'Where?'

'It's only a small job, and they can't afford to pay much.'

'Okay. I'm interested.'

He cleared his throat. 'Don't get upset about this.'

'Quit stalling and tell me.'

'The residents' action group—the group protesting against the Dermont plant—asked if I knew anyone who could help them.'

She froze. How could she work for the residents? Only a few days ago, she'd been on the other side of the fence, countering their efforts. How could she, with a clear conscience, switch sides?

'They want to put together a media kit. You'd know all about the type of stuff they need. They also want leaflets for a letter-box drop in the surrounding area. Other things too, but I'm not sure of the details.'

She hesitated. 'They've got enough money for all of this? I'm talking about production costs, artwork, printing and so on, in addition to my fee.'

He nodded.

'Out of their own pockets?'

He shifted position. 'Mostly. They've had some donations to help set up a fighting fund too.'

His hand went to his jaw and, as he rubbed it, she realised in a flash what he wasn't saying—*he* was paying for their materials. Which made her decision even more difficult. She would be taking Luke's money, indirectly.

'I guarantee you'll like the woman responsible,' Luke said. 'Mary Horton. She's a battler. Feisty.'

Did she want to like Mary? What if she found herself on the opposing side again?

But, seriously, no one needed to know she was involved.

She'd be working in the background, and it wasn't as if she'd ever go back to the firm even if they asked her. She'd never work for Tom Dermont again in any capacity after what he'd done to her. No matter what he offered.

'Tell you what, don't make up your mind yet. Give Mary a call. Or drive down there and see her. Have a chat with her and then decide.'

In truth, she could see nothing to stop her taking the job other than her own guilt. Which was dispersing. Fast. She didn't possess any inside information on Dermont she could pass on, so there was no issue other than her own conscience.

Nodding, she stood, fetched a notepad and wrote down Mary's contact details. 'Okay, I will. I'll ring her later. But, first, I'm going to get changed and see you outside.'

Luke gave her a questioning look.

'You didn't think you were going to have all the fun, did you? It's my garden.'

He smiled. 'Fair enough. You can start the planting.'

Apart from a short break for lunch, they spent the rest of the day working in the garden. Della hadn't had so much fun since they were kids.

'Bad light stops play,' Luke said, walking up behind her as she firmed the soil around the last of the screening shrubs.

She looked towards the house and saw he'd completed paving one terrace. 'It looks great.'

He nodded. 'I'll be back bright and early tomorrow. It will take a full day to do the other one as well as the steps. Then there's the garden edging.' He glanced around at the outlined flower beds. 'Maybe two days more.'

Della looked away. The thought of spending another two days working side by side with a shirtless Luke made her body react in an embarrassing way. She should have less difficulty keeping her hormones under control, now she was a grown woman, but it seemed to be harder than ever.

Was it because she was no longer the inexperienced girl she'd been back when she'd first met Luke? Now she knew what she was missing, and the thought of what it could be like with Luke sent her mind into meltdown.

She gave the ground one last pat while she waited for her cheeks to cool. 'You must be starving,' she said as she got to her feet. 'I think I have some eggs in the fridge. I could whip up an omelette.'

He shook his head. 'You're not cooking tonight. You're exhausted.'

Now he mentioned it, she did hurt in places she didn't know she had. She braced a hand against her back. 'Thanks for reminding me.'

'I could order pizza. If you don't mind me using your shower, I have some clean clothes in the car.'

She blinked. 'Why are you carrying clothes in your car? Have you been thrown out of the hotel?'

He gave her a sheepish smile. 'No, actually, Mum insisted on doing my laundry. I tried to refuse, but…'

'Ah, I see. Well, okay, then. You can have first use of the shower while I tidy up here. Then you can order the pizza while I have my turn which, I predict, will be longer.'

'Deal.'

Later, Luke looked over at his old friend, curled in the corner of a sofa, legs tucked under her while she bit into her fourth—or was it fifth?—slice of pizza. Where did she put it all? With a pang he realised she probably hadn't had much to eat this week. He'd seen the state of her fridge when he'd gone looking for juice while she was in the shower. All he'd found was the lemonade bottle they'd emptied earlier, and hardly anything in the way of food. She'd probably been too busy looking for a job to think about something as unimportant as shopping. He'd offer to help but he doubted she'd let him do more than the garden.

This reminded him of the early years of their friendship when she'd often turned up at his parents' house desperately hungry. Only this time it was *his* fault.

He took another bite of pizza, but it had lost its flavour. Sleepless nights had caused dark smudges on the delicate skin beneath Della's eyes. Also his fault, he supposed.

She'd done well to reach the level she had at the firm, though he imagined she'd earned every iota of success through her own hard work. But was she happy? He didn't think so. In fact, it was as clear as Evian she didn't enjoy dealing with clients like Dermont whose values were so different from her own.

He knew her values. They might have been buried under a driving ambition forged by a deprived childhood, but they were still there, in another level of existence—the real, true, genuine substance of who she was. They were part of the reason he'd felt such a connection with her years ago. Despite their different backgrounds, they'd had the same passions and visions.

Della broke the silence. 'Not hungry?'

He started.

She pointed at the slice of pizza in his hand. 'You've been staring at that for ages. Are you going to eat it or memorise it?'

He gave himself a mental shake and dragged his thoughts back to the here and now. 'Just taking a breather,' he said. 'I can't compete with you when it comes to eating.'

She grimaced. 'I don't know why you ordered so much. Were you expecting reinforcements?'

He shrugged. 'No, just out of practice. I hope there's room in your fridge for the leftovers.' Which he didn't need to ask. He'd banked on filling some of the empty space without hurting her pride. Not the most balanced diet, but, if she didn't get around to shopping over the next few days, at least she'd have reheated pizza.

He began to chew again. They'd managed to get past the hurt and anger he'd inadvertently caused by writing his story, and for that he was immensely grateful.

They'd avoided as if by mutual agreement any mention of the kiss. What he really wanted to do was tell her it had moved him in a way he couldn't remember experiencing in a long time. If ever. But he couldn't say those words, and his heart hit his ribs as he acknowledged that he had to keep them to himself. He could say nothing or he might lose her. With their friendship on a fragile footing, he was determined to tread carefully. Much more carefully. He wasn't going to do anything to risk it again. He'd take his lead from her.

As for her job, he'd hate to see her retreat behind a false persona again, to watch her take on another role that prevented the expression of what she believed. If he could help with that without her knowledge, without hurting her pride, he would.

He'd start by donating money for Mary's promotional products. He'd intended to lend a hand there anyway. Hopefully, Della would see her way clear to take the job.

He had another idea, but he needed to check out some details before he put it on the table.

CHAPTER EIGHT

ON MONDAY, having made an appointment to see Mary Horton that day, Della eyed the newspaper from exactly a week ago, still in its wrapper on the hall table where she'd left it. A lot had happened since she dropped it there on her way out to work. And now, if she was going to be working for the residents' action group, she really should read Luke's story.

Now that the shock of losing her job had subsided, she could cope with whatever emotions the story raised. Besides, she owed it to Luke to read it. He was her friend and it meant a lot to him. He'd never intended to hurt her. She believed him when he said it, and she couldn't blame him for not expecting his actions to have the result they did. If the firm had shown a fraction of the loyalty towards her that she'd shown it during her term of employment, she would still be working there—maybe not on the Dermont account, but in all honesty that would have been no great disappointment.

With a sigh, she carried the newspaper into the kitchen, ripping off the wrapper as she went, then she made a coffee before settling at the table. Ignoring the screaming headline, she began to read.

Several minutes later, she lifted her eyes and stared ahead, not seeing the gorgeous new garden through the French doors.

The tears on her face were about how full and connected she felt. How proud of Luke. Instinct told her that every fact contained in the exposé would have been checked and corroborated, every damning statistic verified.

She'd worked hard on behalf of Tom Dermont. She'd put a positive spin on his provocative statements. She'd deflected media attention from his plant's incidents. And why? Because it was her job, when what she should have been doing was telling the truth. Telling it like it was. As Luke had.

For the first time, she wondered when she'd begun to shut down her true feelings, when she'd stopped being who she used to be.

Had she lost her integrity?

Integrity meant not compromising your belief system. Luke had mentioned a compromised existence—now she understood what he'd tried to say. She might have mislaid her integrity for a while but it was still there. She could find it again.

Feeling a sense of release, she realised she'd been in a state of perpetual weariness from trying to be someone she was not. Now she didn't have to try, and the exhaustion eased immediately.

It was so simple. All she had to do was listen to and respond from the depth of her real self.

What she would do with this knowledge she couldn't say, but she felt as if she'd begun a journey. She could go anywhere she wanted. The choice was up to her.

But first she had to go to Mary Horton's house.

At first sight, Mary Horton looked like a sweet grandmother. After a few minutes in her house, Della knew different. Mary would put most of Della's former colleagues to shame with her knowledge of current affairs, both Australian and international.

It was easy to see why Luke liked her. The home-made shortbread didn't hurt either. Della smiled as Mary made space on the small round table for a pot of tea. To do so, she had to move a pile of books, and as she transferred them to a side table she gestured at a filing cabinet against the wall.

'That's full of reports on incidents. Leaks, in other words. Take a look. The folder on top is an index.'

Della flicked through the index, a thick wad of closely spaced handwritten pages. Slowing, she frowned at the number of lines detailing liquid leaks, gas escapes and other events. She'd had no idea so many had taken place. Tom Dermont hadn't given the impression they'd had anywhere near this number.

'How long have you lived here?' she asked over her shoulder.

'Since the houses were built, dear. Early sixties. And over there was open space.' She gestured towards the window, and Della looked out at the Dermont Chemicals plant directly across the road.

'Don't get me wrong, I'm not anti-industry,' Mary said. 'It funds my retirement, after all. I invest in industrial shares.' She paused to pour out two cups of tea. 'No, what annoys me is the short-sightedness of locating factories like this one cheek by jowl with houses and then refusing to take responsibility for the problems it causes. In those days, of course, it was mostly young families that lived in these homes.'

Della opened the nearest drawer and pulled out a file. Carrying it back to the table, she spread it open on her lap while she took a sip of tea from the china cup Mary had filled.

'So, the houses were here first?'

'Oh, yes. I remember when talk of building an industrial park first began. We expressed our concern, of course, but the government of the day assured us it would be restricted to light industrial use—warehouses and the like. We backed down because there were plenty of young adults who needed jobs around here. Have another shortbread, dear.'

'Thanks.' Della took a buttery triangle from the plate. She hadn't had much other than pizza over the weekend, and she'd only had that because of the amount Luke had ordered on Friday.

'Later, we discovered the local council had given Dermont's a substantial rates concession to move here, and the rest is history.'

As Della bit into her shortbread, her nostrils twitched at an odour drifting in from outside. She wrinkled up her nose and glanced at the window.

'Oh, I'm sorry, dear. It's because I've got the window open. I don't like to have the air conditioning on constantly, especially in spring when the weather's so nice.' She crossed the room and wound a handle to close the window. 'Fresh air is a misnomer in this suburb, of course.'

Della frowned. 'I've been at the plant for meetings,' she said. 'But I've never smelled anything like this.'

Mary nodded. 'Couple of reasons. One, you probably didn't have an appointment when they were venting. I expect Tom Dermont arranges his meetings between times. Two, the offices are on the far side of the factory and the prevailing wind comes this way. Good thinking on their part. Let the residents put up with it instead of the office workers.'

'I suppose so,' Della said. She wondered why she'd never questioned Tom more fully about his operation, but then she hadn't been all that interested in the truth, only in doing her job well. She took a deep breath, huffing out her exasperation with herself. 'Now,' she said. 'Luke told me a bit about the work you want me to do but I'd like to hear it from you, if you don't mind.'

'Ah…Luke.' Mary grinned. 'He's a darling, isn't he?'

Della made a non-committal noise. 'We're old friends.' Her cheeks warmed as Mary studied her, and she had the uncomfortable feeling that Mary could see the full extent of her feelings for him. 'About the media kit...?'

Mary frowned. 'You're sure you can help us? Luke said you might have too much on your plate. I wouldn't like you to feel under an obligation to do this.'

She was grateful that he'd given her the option of backing out gracefully, but it was the last thing she wanted to do. Nodding, she said, 'I'm sure. If you want me, that is.'

'Of course we do. Professionalism is what we've lacked till now. Right, enough chit-chat. This is what I was thinking for the media kit...'

Twenty minutes into her discussion with Mary, just as Della had begun to question which of them was the so-called expert, the chime of the doorbell made her look up from her notes.

'Excuse me while I answer that,' Mary said. 'Have some more shortbread.'

Della did so, and as she ate it her gaze wandered to the view from the window. She couldn't imagine putting up with odours like the one she'd smelled earlier. Having believed Tom when he'd said the residents were complaining about nothing, she felt like an idiot. Quite apart from the toxic leaks, she could see they'd had to put up with a lot of minor inconvenience over the years.

'Look who it is,' Mary said as she re-entered the room. 'Your young man.'

Della swivelled. 'Mary, I told you, we're just friends.'

'Cup of tea, Luke?'

'No, thanks. I came to take you both to lunch.'

Della looked at the shortbread in her hand. 'I don't think I should eat anything else.'

'Oh, don't be silly, Della. Of course we'll go to lunch with Luke. I'm not going to pass up an offer like that from a handsome young man. Just let me fetch my handbag.'

Della sighed. She knew a railroad when she saw one, and there was no point in arguing with the Indian-Pacific. Anyway, lunch with Luke would be good. Now they were friends again, she had no reason to avoid him.

Luke drove them to a beachside bar-restaurant where the three of them sat outside in the shade of a wide umbrella. A soft sea breeze tugged at Della's loose-fitting silk blouse and, after ordering, she leaned against the chair back, leaving Mary and Luke to chat. She enjoyed the spring sun, not harsh enough to burn but warm enough to feel good on her face.

'Gorgeous, aren't they?' Mary said, nodding at the children on the beach below.

Della focused on them. In all the upheaval of losing her job and trying to find a new one, she'd pushed aside the news from Dr Morgan. But it had sat in her subconscious like a splinter, festering. Now, watching this young family, pain reached inside and twisted her gut. It took all her effort to keep her face straight.

Luke gave her a puzzled glance, then twisted to see what they were looking at. 'Talking of children,' he said as he turned back, 'don't you think Lynnie is looking tired?'

Surprised, Della dragged in a breath. She felt a twinge of guilt. If there was something wrong with Lyn, she should have noticed. Being wrapped up in her own problems was no excuse.

'I haven't seen much of her this week, but I imagine she would be tired with two little ones. And Patrick works so hard, he can't help out much.'

'My point exactly. I think we should take the kids off her hands for a day.' Luke told Mary, 'Lyn is my sister and Della's friend.'

'Excuse me?' Della said. 'Did I hear you right—you and I should take out the children?'

'Well, it would make Lyn feel better if you were there to

keep an eye on me, don't you think? We could take them to the park or the zoo or something.'

'A whole day?'

'Half a day seems a bit mean.' He gave a thoughtful nod. 'I reckon that's the way to go, give Lyn a whole day to herself.'

'It's a lovely idea,' Mary said. 'Time to herself, combined with knowing the children are safe. You couldn't give a mother a better gift, in my opinion. She'll be grateful to you both.'

Della looked from Mary to Luke. He smiled, his eyes glinting in the sun like smoked glass. 'Agreed?'

His smile warmed her. She loved that he cared enough to notice Lyn looked tired, and of course she wanted to do her bit to help. 'Agreed. When did you have in mind?'

'I'll let you know when I've arranged it with her, but some time this week?'

'Okay. As long as I can fit it around my work on Mary's leaflets.'

Mary chuckled. 'I've waited nearly forty years, I can wait an extra day or two.'

'But still, when you're paying for something you're entitled to receive it in a timely manner,' Della said.

Mary shrugged. 'Yes, but I'm not—'

'Do you think that's one of those new shark patrols?' Luke interrupted, pointing into the sky above the ocean.

Della looked over her shoulder at the small fixed-wing aircraft, smiling to herself at his abrupt change of subject. He didn't know she'd already worked out who'd financed the work for Mary.

'No, it's not,' Mary said. 'They're not starting till summer.' She paused while their meals were delivered to the table. Once the young waiter had left, she said, 'Did you know there have been more sightings of great white sharks off the beaches of Adelaide in the last two years than in the previous twenty?'

Della and Luke shook their heads.

'One theory is, the tuna farms around Port Lincoln attract them and then they stay near the coast looking for other easy pickings. Another is that they follow the breeding snapper up the coast.'

'Sounds like you've studied the subject,' Luke said.

'Not especially, but I take an interest. I'm all for conservation, and I hate the idea of hunting such magnificent creatures, but I do worry about our young people. They love their surfing, don't they? And who can blame them, when we have such beautiful beaches?'

While Luke questioned Mary further, Della ate her food and let her gaze drift to the beach again, watching the young family pack up its belongings.

She had a cold pit of despair in the base of her stomach whenever she thought about her infertility. But she'd have to get used to seeing young families like this one, to seeing what she couldn't have.

'How long have you two known each other?' Mary asked.

Della glanced at Luke. 'Too long,' she said with a grimace. 'Makes me feel old to think about it.'

Luke grinned. 'We met when I was fifteen and Della was…' He raised his eyebrows at her. 'Fourteen?'

'Yes.' She nodded. 'The same age as Lyn. I became friends with Lyn first, but Luke kept hanging around with us,' she told Mary, lowering her voice as if sharing a confidence. 'We tried to shake him but he wouldn't take the hint.'

Mary laughed. 'I can imagine. He's a determined one, isn't he?'

CHAPTER NINE

'So, you and Luke are friends again?' Lyn said the next day.

Della rolled her eyes at the phone. 'Of course. Don't tell me you doubted it?'

Lyn laughed. 'I knew you'd get over it. It was just a matter of how long it would take you to realise Luke did you a favour.'

'Yeah, right.'

'I mean it. Now you'll have more time for your friends.'

Fingers of guilt poked Della. 'I am a lousy friend, aren't I?'

'Oh, come off it. I was only joking.'

'No, it's true. I should help you out with the children, make sure you're getting your rest.'

'Well, on that subject, Luke just left. He came here determined to kidnap my children.'

'Kidnap?'

'Borrow. He said the two of you wanted to take them out for the day.'

'You did agree, didn't you?'

'Of course I did. Why would I knock back such an offer? I'm going to the hairdresser's, and then I'll have a facial and a manicure. That's just for starters. It'll be lovely, but I don't understand what's got into you both.'

'We both think you need an opportunity to pamper yourself.'

'Great, but—'

'Luke wants to act the adoring uncle.' More to the point, he couldn't see a problem without trying to fix it.

'Oh, well, I suppose he does have some time to make up for. I don't want to sound as if I don't appreciate the offer. I do, of course.'

'You're welcome.'

'Isn't it a shame Luke and his wife didn't have children? He'd make a wonderful father. Don't you agree?'

'Yes,' Della said, closing her eyes.

'Provided that he'd settle down long enough to be a proper father anyway. I hope he finds someone else soon and they start a family before he gets too old to enjoy it.'

Della's breath caught in her throat. She leaned forward, her forehead pressing against the wall. Lyn wouldn't condone a relationship between Della and Luke, knowing, as she did, that Della could never give her brother the family he should have. She might not express her disappointment, but Della would always know how she felt.

Not that it was worth worrying about, when Della knew she herself could never allow a relationship to happen.

'Dell, hon? Are you there? I haven't upset you have I, Dell, with all this talk of children?'

'No,' she croaked. 'Course not.'

'It shouldn't be too hard for Luke to find someone else,' Lyn said. 'He's not bad looking, is he?'

'No, he's not.' Good enough to make her nerves prickle when he came near. Clothes certainly did not make the man— ancient jeans or designer dinner-suit, whatever he wore he sent her stomach into freefall.

'I wonder if I could find an available woman who'd suit him. There are some single doctors at Patrick's hospital. It might be worth a thought.'

'Lyn, you know Luke won't thank you for matchmaking.

He didn't like it when we were teenagers. Anyway, I'm not sure he's over Yvonne yet.'

Lyn sighed. 'No, you're right. So, what about you, have you found a new job yet?'

'No, but I'm doing some freelance work. It will cover this month's mortgage repayment.'

'Great. Perhaps you should set yourself up to do freelance stuff on a long-term basis? It's better than doing a job you hate like the last one.'

Frowning, Della said, 'What makes you think I hated it?'

Lyn clicked her tongue. 'That came out wrong. Sorry. But now you can find a job you *really* like. Oh, I know you were doing well and in line for a big promotion and so on, but you weren't *happy,* were you? Be honest now.'

Della hesitated. 'I did have a problem with some of the clients, only I didn't realise how big a problem.'

'And you do now?'

'Yes. I think so.'

'That's good, because I didn't like to see you ignoring your true gifts and talents.'

Blinking, Della said, 'Which are?'

'Well...empathy. You were always good at seeing both sides of a story and understanding where someone was coming from.'

Della tilted her head. 'You think so?'

'Mmm-hmm. The question is, what are you going to do now you've worked out what you shouldn't be doing?'

'That's the problem. I don't know. I feel a kind of emptiness. Nothingness. I had these goals, and now suddenly I don't. I feel like I've woken up from a long sleep and I'm disoriented.'

Lyn let out a low whistle. 'Dell, hon, I think I know what you mean. It's like you've been living life to a script and the director just ripped it up and threw it away.

'All I can say, Dell, is listen to your gut. Let your instincts show you what to do next.' She groaned. 'Bugger. Cassie's crying. I thought I might get a longer break than this. Oh, well, I'll have a long one tomorrow, won't I? Can't wait. I'd better go. Hope she doesn't cause you too much trouble tomorrow. See you.'

Della stood with the phone pressed against her chest after Lyn had hung up. She would like a job that made her feel she was doing something worthwhile. Trouble was, she was hamstrung by her mortgage and other commitments. Freelancing was unlikely to bring in enough to meet them. As it was, it looked like she'd have to let the car go. She pouted. Her lovely car. It would be a wrench, but she had no choice.

She gave herself a mental shake. If she had to let go of material things…tough. At least she'd have her pride. She could start again. She'd built her life up from nothing before and she'd do it again. Only, this time, she'd make better life choices.

Returning to the leaflet she was working on for Mary, she forced herself to focus. She wanted to feel she'd earned her money.

Luke's money.

She rolled her eyes. She was doing the right thing working for Mary. Whose money had paid for it was irrelevant.

When Luke collected Della the next morning, she was ready to go and looking forward to the day.

'Have you decided on somewhere to take the kids?' she asked.

'Well, Lyn said the simpler the better. Apparently, Jamie likes nothing better than kicking a soccer ball, but Patrick never has time to take him to the park. And you know what their garden is like,' he said with a grimace.

Della did. Japanese style. Patrick's choice. 'I'm surprised

Lyn doesn't put her foot down with Patrick over it,' she said. 'It's no good for kids.'

'Mmm. Talking of gardens, how's yours?'

'Alive. I hope I can keep it that way. At least the plants will have a chance to make a root system before the hot weather arrives. A few weeks later and they might not have survived the summer.'

'Right. I chose a good time to be a moron, then?'

She smiled. If there was anyone less like a moron, she'd never met him. She was saved from having to answer as he manoeuvred into a parking space outside Lyn's house. Lyn was waiting for them and they swapped cars, Luke taking the keys to her sensible four-wheel-drive complete with baby and child seats. Lyn got into his Saab with a broad smile on her face.

'This is more like it,' she called through the open window. 'I'm off. I'll keep my mobile switched on in case there's a problem.'

'There's confidence,' Luke said.

'You can't blame her,' Della said, waving Lyn off. 'She's a mum. It's her job to worry.'

She finished strapping Cassie into the baby seat while Luke loaded up the back of the vehicle with the picnic basket and blanket he'd taken from his own car, a pram and Jamie's collection of balls.

'And this,' Jamie called, picking up a bundle of sticks.

'What is it?' Luke asked.

'My kite. But Mummy couldn't put it together so she said you'd do it.'

'Uh-huh.' Luke grinned at Della as she joined him at the rear of the car. 'This is going to be great.'

She smiled back. 'I hope you still think so by the end of the day.'

He draped an arm around her shoulders. 'Don't worry.

We're going to have a good time. Just you, me and the kids. Like a proper family.'

A chill ran through her. She didn't respond, and he squeezed her shoulders before returning to the loading. Of all the things he could have said, few would have grated at her raw nerves like those words.

'Okay. Into the car,' Luke said.

Inside, Jamie had plenty to say and Della only had to make interested noises. By the time they reached Hazelwood Park, she'd composed herself again.

At first, the three of them played a triangular game of soccer, with Cassie watching happily from the pram, but when Cassie became restless Della detached herself from the game and walked her from one end of the memorial garden to the other, the scent of lavender thrilling her as she passed the massed planting. The antics of Rosella parrots in the huge Moreton Bay fig tree overhead made her smile, and she paused so Cassie could see the others foraging on the ground.

When the sun emerged from behind a bank of white cloud, Della retrieved a sun hat from the well-packed bag, popped it on Cassie's head and played an impromptu game of peek-a-boo. Then she pushed her across the grass to the small lake formed by damming the natural creek. She was still crouching by the pram, cooing over ducks on the pool, when Luke and Jamie joined them at the water's edge.

'It must be feeding time,' Luke said as he dropped to the ground beside her.

'For you or the ducks?'

He held up half a loaf of bread. 'Do I come prepared or what?'

'I repeat, for you or the ducks?'

'Ducks,' Jamie said, holding his hand out for some bread.

Luke broke off a chunk and handed it to him. 'Break off little pieces, mate. Don't throw it all at once. You might hit a duck on the head and knock it out.' Jamie giggled and Luke knelt beside him, pointing out the ducks who'd missed out each time so Jamie could aim his next throw towards them.

Della bit her lip. Typical—always looking out for the underdog—duck—whatever. He was such a generous, thoughtful guy. She'd never met anyone better. She never would.

'Can we fly the kite now, Uncle Luke?' Jamie tossed the remaining bread into the water and rushed off to fetch the kite. Luke followed.

When Cassie began to grizzle, Della lifted her to her shoulder, cuddling her till she calmed. Slowly, she strolled to where Luke and Jamie had assembled the kite and were attempting to launch it into the air. After several attempts, it finally soared high, and Jamie squealed.

'Look,' he shouted. 'I'm flying it.'

'Great.' She didn't know who looked most excited, Jamie or Luke, and she grinned at each in turn.

She watched for a while, rocking Cassie, laughing when the wind picked up and the kite dragged Jamie along the ground until Luke could convince him to hand it over. Then she placed a sleeping Cassie back into the pram, pushed it into the shade of a tree and spread the picnic rug alongside.

With perfect timing, Luke and Jamie arrived just as she finished unpacking the lunch.

'I have a favour to ask,' Luke said as he took a sandwich from the plastic box.

She looked at him, her eyes narrowing. 'What is it?'

'Don't look so worried.' He took a swig of water from a small bottle. 'I need a date for a function. No big deal.'

His tone was casual, so why did she get the impression her answer was important to him? She tilted her head and gazed at him for a moment longer.

'All right,' she said. 'I'll go with you. What is it? A media back-slapping fest?'

'No. It's a charity fund-raiser.'

'The charity you work for?'

'Yes. And thanks. I think you'll enjoy it.'

She turned to persuade Jamie to sit down while he ate.

'How did you get to be so good with kids?' he said.

She shrugged. 'I don't think I am particularly good with them.'

'I remember how you used to help Mum with Megan and Poppy. Lyn wasn't any help at all. Too interested in curling her hair—or was it straightening? Either way, she was too busy. Yet, you always had time to help with the littlies.'

'They were so cute. I was envious of Lyn having sisters.'

He nodded. 'Do you still envy her, having children when you don't?'

She sucked in a short breath and felt her heart thump in her chest. For an instant she thought he knew the truth, and she didn't think she could cope with that.

'What's wrong, Shrimp?' His expression puzzled, he leaned closer.

He didn't know.

'Nothing,' she said before taking a long, slow breath. Conscious of Jamie sitting on the far edge of the blanket, she spoke softly. 'So, was this day out more about you missing the children at the orphanage than about helping Lyn?'

A range of emotions crossed his face before he answered. 'I hadn't given it conscious thought, but you might be right. I must be more selfish than I realised.'

'Selfish? You're not selfish.' She watched him, lost in thought, and emotion clogged her throat. Surprising herself, she leaned forward to place a light kiss on his lips.

He stared at her as she straightened, his eyes darker than normal.

He cleared his throat. 'What was that for?'

'To say "thank you".'

'For?'

She swallowed. 'For being the most unselfish person I know.'

He looked troubled. 'That's not true. Far from it. There have been so many times...I cared too much about myself in the past. About protecting myself.'

She watched him for a long moment before making a decision. 'Do you think I'm selfish too?'

'God, no.'

'Well, I know all about protecting myself. I wouldn't have survived my childhood if I hadn't.'

'Della...' He shifted closer, reaching out a hand to rub her forearm. 'You're not comparing apples with apples.'

'It's the same. We've both been through trauma. Different types of trauma, I grant you, but the effects are the same.'

He shook his head. 'I was a grown man. You were a child.'

'We can't control the things that happen to us at any age. We can't control external events. All we can control is our internal reactions to those events, the reactions that we carry with us long term.'

'But what if we're ashamed of our internal reactions?'

'Then we change them.'

He pushed a hand through his hair. 'Della, it's not that simple.'

'But it is. I told you I'd forgiven my parents. How do you think I did that?'

'I have no idea.'

'In my head, I gave them permission to be the way they were. I accepted that the way they were had nothing to do with me. I stopped taking it personally. Then I went back over my reactions to the things they did and changed them. Instead of hating my parents, I ended up pitying them.'

She paused to take a drink. Her throat felt raw. She wasn't used to talking about such intimate stuff. She wouldn't have talked about it now if it hadn't been for the fact that Luke needed to know. She turned back to him, but he was staring into the distance, his eyes shining. With tears? He blinked and turned his eyes to meet hers.

'I understand. But it's different in my case. And it's not easy.'

'Of course it's not easy. It wasn't easy for me, either, but you need to give yourself permission to see things differently. You couldn't fix the horrors you saw so you thought you'd failed. But you didn't fail. You brought all that injustice to the public's attention. You did what you set out to do. You need to accept that you did the best you could in the circumstances.'

She looked at Jamie who was yawning noisily. 'Sleepy?'

'No.' He shook his head, but his drooping eyelids told her otherwise.

'He normally has a sleep around this time,' she said to Luke. 'And Cassie will sleep for a while yet, I should think. What shall we do? We can't go back to Lyn's yet. She won't be home anyway. I guess we could go to your parents' house. It's closer than mine.'

'No, they're not home either. Let's go to the hotel. He can sleep in my room.'

She frowned. 'In your hotel room?'

'Yes. He only needs a bed, doesn't he?'

Nodding, she began to pack away the picnic, and Luke helped.

'You didn't answer my question earlier,' Luke said. 'Do you envy Lyn? Do you want children of your own?'

'No, definitely not.'

She was surprised to hear how firm her voice came out, considering the quivering inside her. She took another breath. 'In fact, I can't imagine anything worse.'

'Sorry?'

After staring at her for a long moment, he said, 'But why? You're a natural with kids.' He gestured towards Jamie and Cassie. 'And they love you.'

Telling Luke she was a failure as a woman felt like an entirely different matter from confiding in Lyn. She couldn't do it. Instead, she lowered her voice, not wanting to risk Jamie understanding. 'Oh, it's fine playing the auntie. I can hand them back afterwards.' She wiped her palms across each other to reinforce her words.

'Really?' His voice resonated with disbelief.

'Besides, I can like children without wanting my own. I have my career to think about,' she said. 'I wouldn't want to be distracted from it.'

'You wouldn't have to give it up. Thousands of women work and raise children.'

'I know, but it's not for me. Seriously, Luke, I have no desire to burden myself with kids.'

'Burden? I never expected to hear you say this.'

And she didn't like lying to him but, right now, she preferred it to the alternative. She'd tell him the truth one day, but not yet. She still needed time to accustom herself to it.

'Did you and Yvonne disagree about children?' She looked at him as she asked the question, and saw him stiffen.

'Yes.'

'You wanted them and she didn't?'

'Yes.' He stood, picking up the picnic basket and gathering Jamie's soccer balls into his other arm.

'And that was a deal breaker?'

'Yes.' With a frozen expression, he headed towards the car.

She sighed. How ironic that his wife didn't want his children, while Della would love to be able to have his children and couldn't. The knowledge made her even more determined not to reveal her feelings for him. She couldn't even think about a relationship beyond what they had now.

She couldn't give him the family he wanted, and she couldn't risk losing him because of it.

Jamie was asleep by the time Luke parked the car and Cassie still hadn't woken so, between the two of them, they carried both children up to the hotel room.

Luke stood back and watched as Della slipped the shoes off the sleeping boy and covered both children with a sheet. She gave each of them a light kiss before turning from the bed with a smile.

He wasn't fooled by the rubbish she'd spouted at the park about not wanting children. Blind Freddie could see she had an instinct to nurture, and always had. He clearly remembered the way she'd looked out for his little sisters. She was a natural.

'How long do you think they'll sleep?' he asked.

'I don't know. I think Jamie usually goes to bed for an hour in the afternoon. Cassie should wake before then. She'll need feeding.'

'Shall we have a coffee while we wait?'

'Sure.'

He pulled the kettle and coffee-making paraphernalia from the cupboard at the far end of the hotel room.

He was confused. Since he'd made the mistake of kissing her, he'd tried not to think of Della as anything but his friend. But, the more he tried, the more difficult it became.

He sneaked a sideways look at her standing in front of the floor-to-ceiling windows. Her bare shoulders drew his gaze. They made him want to walk up behind her and slide his hands under the thin white straps which were their only covering. To stroke the pale golden skin, then let his finger-tips trail down her arms until his fingers entwined with hers. To press his lips against the tempting nape of her neck, and with the tip of his tongue—

The kettle clicked off and he jumped like an idiot, before snatching at it as steam spurted from the spout. God, what was the matter with him?

Hmm. The answer was obvious. And now he had to think pure thoughts while his blood cooled down.

CHAPTER TEN

DELLA turned from the window when she heard Luke behind her. Taking her coffee from him with a smile of thanks, she looked at the sofa. Luckily, it wasn't an overgrown armchair masquerading as a sofa. There was plenty of room for two.

'Do you want to watch television?' Luke asked.

'No. Unless you do?'

He shook his head.

She sat carefully, balancing the scalding coffee. 'What did you miss most about home during the years you were away?'

He blew out a breath as he took a seat next to her. 'Tough question. You mean, apart from you, right?'

'As if,' she said with an eye roll.

He grinned. 'I did miss you. Especially in the early years. I was pretty lonely there for a while. I missed the stuff we used to do.'

There, in a nutshell, was the huge discrepancy between their feelings. Understandably, he'd missed the camaraderie of his former life once thrust into an unfamiliar situation. She, on the other hand, had struggled to go on living after having her heart wrenched from her body.

No comparison.

She had to swallow hard before she could speak again. 'You couldn't have been lonely for too long. You got married.'

His face fell. 'Right.'

'Tell me about her,' she said softly.

He started. 'Hmm?'

'Tell me about your wife. About Yvonne.'

'What do you want to know?'

She gave a small shrug. 'I don't know. Anything. I didn't have time to get to know her when you brought her over here. All I know is what she looked like.'

He stared as if he could see through the walls of the hotel room. She watched as his eyes lost their focus. When he spoke, she steeled herself to hear about his love for the other woman.

'It was the way she looked that attracted me to her. As you know, she had the most amazing red hair. Long curls, right down to her waist. It shone in the sun. Shimmered.' He shook his head. 'Fantastic.'

Della fought to stifle the jealousy that threatened to bubble up and overwhelm her. She had to maintain her control, keep her face straight. She needed her mask, the one she wore to pretend she felt nothing.

Luke turned to face her. 'In fact, it was fake.'

'Her hair?'

'The colour.' He gave her a lopsided grin. 'Fooled me. But then, she fooled me in lots of ways. I was the biggest fool you could ever meet.'

'No.'

'Yes. She only had to twitch her little finger and I ran. She had me feeling like I was on fire.'

'Oh,' Della croaked.

'Oh, yeah. I was in deep.' He rolled his eyes. 'Love's a weird thing. It completely wrecks your thought processes. It's like a virus that destroys your rational self. There's no cure. All you can do is wait for your antibodies to do their work and gradually gain the upper hand.'

She blinked at his cynicism. 'And yours did?'

'Gain the upper hand? Eventually.' He shrugged. 'Actually, the whole sorry business was over in a ridiculously short time.'

His gaze wandered into the distance again, and she waited patiently for him to go on. She knew he would. It sounded like he was talking about this part of his life for the first time. Now he'd made the effort to start, he would finish.

'We'd only known each other for four weeks when we married. One month. That's how fast we fell for each other. Or, maybe I should say, how fast I fell for her. She was so sexy. So exotic. The most beautiful woman I'd ever known.'

Della bit her lip to keep from making a sound. She couldn't let him know how much it hurt to hear this.

'We couldn't get enough of each other. Crazy, passionate sex.' He refocused on Della. 'Hey, I'm sorry. I shouldn't be telling you this stuff.'

'No, don't worry.' She flapped a hand. 'I asked, didn't I? And it's not as if I'm an innocent, you know.' She lowered her eyes to her coffee as she took another sip.

He tilted his head and looked at her for a long moment. 'I suppose not. You must have had plenty of men, looking like you do.'

She gave a low laugh. 'Heaps.' *Yeah, right.*

His jaw clenched and unclenched.

She sighed. 'No, not heaps. But there have been a few.'

Something flashed across his eyes. She didn't have time to define it before it was gone. Then he gave her a sad smile.

'It fizzled. The fire. It went out.'

Della curled the fingers of one hand around the edge of the sofa cushion and hung on. 'It did?'

'At first, I didn't want to let her out of my sight. But I had to, of course. Work demands intervened right after the honeymoon. Which was when the problems started.'

Della twisted to place her cup on a side table.

'There were times, after I'd done a story, that sex was the last thing I wanted.'

She swung back to face him.

'You heard right,' he said with a rueful smile. 'Very un-macho admission, I know.'

'No, it's not. After what you'd seen...'

'Turned out it wasn't me she couldn't get enough of, it was sex.'

'That's...dreadful.'

He shrugged. 'The point is, we hardly knew each other when we got married. If we'd taken the time to get ac-quainted, we'd have found out we had some deep-seated dif-ferences. We disagreed on basic issues. As you said, deal breakers.'

Like having children.

Della looked away. Luke had a right to believe he knew her well since they'd been friends for so long, and yet he didn't know about this fundamental flaw in her.

'I shouldn't have married her but...love messes with your head.'

She asked the question she'd wondered about since his return. 'Do you still love her?'

He stretched his arms, then linked his hands behind his head and stared straight ahead. 'No. The end happened suddenly, as suddenly as it had started. I looked at her one day and couldn't stand the sight of her. I realised I didn't love her any more.'

She stared at his rigid profile. 'You know, that sounds more like infatuation than love.' Infatuation that had burnt itself out. Not the long, slow burn of love like she had for him.

He was silent for a moment. 'Yeah, you might be right. Thing is, when you fall in love, how can you tell the difference?'

'Real love is different.' She coughed when emotion rose up to clog her throat. 'I might be wrong. It's not my place to judge. But, from where I sit, it doesn't sound like you really loved your wife.'

He'd turned to look at her. There was no anger in his expression, just curiosity. She summoned the courage to go on.

'Real love is solid. It lasts and lasts, no matter what disagreements come up. A lifetime, at least. It survives separation. It—' She stopped. She was getting too personal now.

He stared for a moment longer. 'How do you know so much about it? Have you been in love, Shrimp?'

She stood and walked to the window where she wrapped her arms around her waist. 'Yes,' she said softly, finding it easier to say with her back to him.

'Are you still in love?'

After a moment's hesitation, she said, 'No,' more softly still. Luke was quiet.

Cassie broke the silence with a gurgle, and Della was grateful. She moved purposefully to the bed and, soon after she'd fed and changed Cassie, Jamie woke up too.

'Shall we go to the beach?' Luke asked. 'I know a nice little house down there.'

'Not so little,' she said. 'It's the perfect size for a fa—' Della fussed with the buttons on Cassie's suit.

Luke came to sit on the edge of the bed where she was kneeling. 'Did you see yourself having a family when you bought it?'

She avoided his intense gaze. 'No, of course not. I was about to regurgitate real-estate jargon. Anyway, we'd like to go to the beach, wouldn't we, Jamie?'

The little boy agreed.

'Lyn's packed for every eventuality. There's bound to be some bathers in the bag,' Della said. 'There are spare shorts, at least.'

Luke grabbed a few items of his own, shoved them into a bag, and they set off.

Later, Della looked across at Luke and Jamie building sandcastles together and decided coming to the beach had been a bad idea. Luke in shorts and nothing else. Did she have a masochistic streak or what?

She'd changed into shorts and a tank top. The day was warm but not warm enough to tempt her to swim in the sea. She'd need a serious heatwave before she'd venture in above her knees.

'Hey! Did you see last night's news?' she said to Luke. 'Did you see Mary leading a protest at the front gate of the Dermont's plant?'

He sat back on his heels. 'Yes. She gave Tom Dermont a tough time, didn't she?'

'Oh, boy, did she ever, but he asked for it.' Della shook her head. 'I don't know what they were thinking, to let him near a microphone.'

'It's about time people got to hear his real opinion instead of the cleaned-up version.'

'Don't get me wrong,' she said. 'I'm on the residents' side now. All I'm saying is—'

'That he's lacking a good PR person?'

'Exactly.'

Luke smiled. 'Well, it serves him right, doesn't it?'

'Sure does.'

Luke nudged Jamie. 'Race you to the water,' he said, and jumped to his feet.

She watched him run in slow motion, letting Jamie race ahead. He would be a great father. Some day he'd have a family of his own and she'd be as jealous as hell. A sigh broke from her. But she'd cope. She'd have to, because he deserved to be a father. It was just that thinking about someone else as the mother of his children made her heart ache.

God, he looked gorgeous. She wanted to slide her hands all over his flexing muscles. All over his body. To feel the hard bits and the soft bits and everything in between. She shook her head as she stood. She had to stop thinking this way. In fact, she had to put an end to these fantasies altogether.

Sighing, she lifted a bubble-blowing Cassie onto her hip and began a slow stroll to the water's edge, enjoying the cool, squidgy sand between her toes.

Dangling Cassie's feet in the little wavelets near the edge, Della was unprepared for the splash which sent water over one leg, wetting her shorts. Straightening, she wiped stray drops of saltwater from Cassie's face, then gave Jamie a mock glare.

'Was that you?'

He squealed and waded deeper, out of her reach.

She followed him, scooped up a handful of water and retaliated. With the exuberance of a four-year-old, Jamie took up the challenge, and within seconds her shorts were drenched.

Luke took Cassie from her arms. 'I don't like to see you at a disadvantage. Now you can go for it.'

And she did, splashing Jamie till he was laughing so much he could hardly keep his footing.

'I'm glad you didn't wear bathers,' Luke said in a low voice, for her ears only.

She looked down. Her white top was so wet her cold nipples were clearly visible through the thin white fabric. They became even tighter as she thought of Luke watching. She looked up and her breath stuck in her throat. There was no mistaking the message in his glinting grey eyes. She received it loud and clear, and sent it straight back with bells on.

Then she remembered where she was and broke eye contact.

'I'll go and get dry,' she said, wading forward to take Cassie from him. 'We'll go back to the house and wait for you boys there.'

Luke watched Della go. He knew he shouldn't have said

a word, but desire for her had been building all day. And then, when he had blurted out what he was thinking, there'd been an answering gleam in her eyes. He could almost see sparks crackling in the air between them while she'd held his gaze.

He could only hope he hadn't upset her. But, God, it was difficult to know what to do. He wanted her so much, but he was terrified that telling her would mean the end of their friendship.

After they'd dropped Jamie and Cassie back to a grateful Lyn, Luke drove Della home. He glanced at Della from time to time. She stayed silent throughout the journey, but she didn't look unhappy. From what he could see, she had a serene smile on her face as she gazed through the window.

Once he'd brought the car to a standstill, she turned to him. 'Thanks for the day. It was a good idea. I enjoyed it.'

'Me too.'

As one hand reached for the door, he touched her other hand. 'Wait.'

She looked back expectantly and suddenly he couldn't hold back any longer. He cupped her face with both hands.

'Della, sweetheart...'

Her eyes widened, and he saw the muscles in her throat contract. He leaned forward and pressed his lips to hers. He kept the contact light. He didn't want there to be any pressure—physical or emotional.

Her eyes opened and he saw the question in them. 'You're wondering whether I meant that as a friend?'

She gave a single nod.

'I didn't.'

He heard her gasp as he withdrew his hands and retreated to his side of the car. 'I'm not going to put any pressure on you, Della, but you need to think about what you want to do.'

'Do?'

'About us.'

CHAPTER ELEVEN

ARRIVING at the Convention Centre on Luke's arm for the second time, Della glanced around the foyer. She recognised a few people, but they were members of Adelaide's A-list mainly, not acquaintances.

She hadn't seen Luke since Wednesday, and when he'd first arrived at her house they'd both been tense, but he seemed perfectly normal as he led her through the crowd and she relaxed too. Unlike the last time, she had no responsibilities tonight and she intended to enjoy herself. She'd done more than enough thinking.

Inside the function room, she ran an experienced eye over the tables and decorative touches. All nicely done in a navy blue and silver theme. Event planning had been one facet of her job she'd particularly enjoyed, especially in the last few days before a function when adrenalin levels were high.

She was surprised when they sat at a table right at the front within a few steps of the stage. Such premium space was usually reserved for VIP's and organisers. Four of the ten seats were taken, and Luke surprised her again by introducing her to the charity's president, its chief executive and their respective partners.

'I feel ignorant,' she whispered to Luke as a waiter circled the table filling water glasses. 'I should have found out more about the charity so I could talk to these people about the work it does.'

'Don't worry. You'll see a video soon. You'll learn plenty from it.'

She lifted her eyebrows. She'd thought they were just coming along to make up the numbers, but she must have underestimated Luke's involvement in the function. How else would he know the running order? She didn't have time to question him further as the evening's MC arrived, along with his stunning wife, to take a seat at the table. A local television personality, he immediately engaged Luke in conversation.

The seat next to Della remained vacant, and just as she'd decided it would stay that way a heavily pregnant woman puffed up to the table. A man trailed behind, frowning.

'Oh boy,' she said, dragging out the chair next to Della. 'I need to sit down.'

'Luke,' the man said, interrupting his conversation. 'Please tell Tanya there's nothing else she can do.'

Luke beamed at the new arrivals. 'Tanya, you've done a fantastic job. Now stop.'

Tanya smiled back at him. 'I just want everything to be perfect for you.'

'It is. No one could have done it better.'

'Thank you,' she said, tugging a tissue from her pocket and dabbing her eyes. 'Now look what you've done. You should know better than to be nice to a pregnant woman. Hormones.'

Della, bemused, gave Luke a questioning look.

'Sorry,' he said. 'Let me introduce you.'

Tanya turned out to be the charity's fund-raising manager. She'd organised the event almost single-handedly. Della understood her anxiety regarding its success, but she hardly had a chance to sympathise as Tanya chattered non-stop.

Entrées arrived and Tanya excused herself. Checking her

watch, she gave a discreet signal to the audio-visual staff, then struggled out of her seat to tap the MC on the shoulder.

Della watched, fascinated and a little envious. Music made her turn her head towards the stage as the MC made his way to the microphone. After a brief welcome speech, he introduced the short film they were to see, and the lights dimmed.

Luke's hand covered Della's where it rested on the table. Her breath caught as his fingers curled under hers, her belly tingling at his touch.

She turned her attention to the screen as the film began. It profiled an orphanage. Two hundred and fifty boys and fifty girls, aged from six to eighteen, called the orphanage home. They had a primary school, a medical centre, a sports field, vegetable garden, and a computer lab. All thanks to the charity's efforts.

Della watched, tears prickling her eyes, as the children's faces filled the screen with their smiles. Most of them had been street beggars, she learned, but by the time they left the orphanage at the age of eighteen they'd either have the skills to find a job or the qualifications needed to go to college.

She blinked as the lights came up and turned to Luke. 'I can see why you wanted to work with those children. They're adorable.'

The MC, returning to his seat, interrupted. 'Good film, Luke,' he said. 'You did a good job.'

Her eyes widened. 'You made the film too?' She supposed it made sense, with his experience.

'Yes, I did,' he said. His eyes followed the charity president, a lady named Phyllis, as she rose from the table and walked towards the stage.

At the same time, she saw Tanya make a subtle signal, and music poured from the speakers again. Phyllis took possession of the microphone centre-stage.

'As our valued supporters, many of you know that our

chief executive is about to retire,' Phyllis said. She nodded in the direction of their table and Della glanced at the balding man she'd been introduced to earlier. He smiled and raised a hand to the room in a brief wave.

'I'm going to ask Christopher to come up here and speak to you all about his time in charge. I'm sure you'll find what he has to say very interesting. I know we have benefited from his experience and ability.

'More about Christopher in a moment. Firstly, I'd like to take this opportunity to announce the appointment of Christopher's successor. He's a man who has everything— the passion, the commitment, the experience and the skills to take this charity forward.

'He is not going to speak tonight because he refuses to steal Christopher's thunder. However, I have to say, as our regional director in south Asia for the last few years—he has worked wonders. Indeed, the orphanage in the short film you saw this evening is a direct result of his own efforts. And, in a large part, to his own financial contribution.

'He'll kill me if I say much more, so I'll leave it to Plato, ancient Greek philosopher, to say it more eloquently: "the measure of a man is what he does with power."'

'Luke Brayford, ladies and gentlemen.'

Della sat, stunned, as a spotlight picked out Luke at her side. He stood, waved, then sat down again and the spotlight withdrew. She hadn't expected this.

Christopher made his way to the stage while Della leaned in to Luke.

'Why didn't you tell me?'

He smiled. 'I wanted to surprise you. Look, when Christopher finishes his speech, let's go outside for some fresh air and I'll explain.'

Della nodded, then sat back and listened to Christopher. She tried to concentrate on what he was saying but her mind kept sliding back to Luke. The warm glow in her chest had to be pride in her old friend. She'd always known he was special, but the shock of hearing *how* special did things to her insides. On top of this, lay the knowledge that he'd decided to take the job. Which meant he'd be staying around. Staying in her life.

Only now did she realise how much she'd hoped he would decide to stay.

At the end of Christopher's speech, Phyllis returned to the microphone to announce the beginning of the auction. Items of celebrity memorabilia would be auctioned off, and Della had no doubt they'd raise a significant amount of cash.

Luke pushed back his chair and offered his hand. She took it and went with him to the foyer, where they found a small sofa in a secluded alcove.

Della sank into the soft leather seat with a sigh. 'When did you make your decision? And do you think you'll be able to settle? What about the children?'

He looked into her eyes as he sat down. 'I was still unde-cided until Wednesday.'

His words brought a blush to her cheeks but she made no response.

'I've talked it over with Phyllis, and I'm going to fly over there several times a year to see the kids. I'll do a mini-tour each time I go, check how things are going at the grass roots.'

'Sounds good, but will that be enough for you?'

He nodded. 'It will have to be. For now, anyway.'

'I'm so proud of you. I didn't realise the charity was based here.'

'It wasn't, but I'm moving Head Office here. It's no big deal with today's technology.'

'What about Phyllis? Where is her office?'

'Melbourne, but it's not a problem. She's a figurehead. She

spends very little time at the office. When we need to meet, I'll go to her.'

'Okay. What about office space? And staff? Do you have all that under control?'

'I haven't been lazing around since I got here. I'm signing the lease on an office on Monday.'

Her eyes widened. 'Oh. I had no idea you were looking.'

'As for staff, I want to talk to you on the subject.'

'Me?'

'My most urgent need is a replacement for Tanya.'

'During maternity leave?'

'No. She's not coming back. She's going to start her own event-planning business in Melbourne. So, I'll need someone to do the publicity, fund-raising, events and so on. What do you think?'

'You want me to find you someone?'

'No.' His mouth twitched into a smile. 'Will you take the job?'

'Me!' Her mind raced. It was exactly the kind of job she'd love. A chance to make a difference. But...

'I can't work for you. I can't have you as my boss.'

'I was thinking more of us as a team. Don't you think we'd be good together?'

'Yes, but...'

'But what?' He reached towards her, brushing the back of his knuckles down her cheek. 'Don't let me down, Shrimp. I need you.'

She swallowed. She'd be working for an organisation she could believe in. The job itself would be great. A sense of freedom swept through her—the freedom to choose. This job was meant for her.

'All right,' she said.

'*Yes.*' Leaning forward, he brushed warm lips across hers.

She sucked in a breath. 'You know what that was?'

'Nice?'

'Sexual harassment. You're my boss.'

He laughed softly. 'Not yet.'

'We have a verbal contract.'

He traced a fingertip around the edge of her ear, then cupped her cheek.

A shiver started in her toes.

'That too,' she said. 'All touching is bad.'

'Really? Do you want me to stop?' He bent his head again. 'Say the word and I'll stop, Della.' His breath tickled her slick lips.

'Don't stop,' she said, and it came out like a whimper.

His kiss was slow and gentle, but she could feel its effects right through her body. Being so close to him, knowing he was everything she'd ever believed and more, made her skin heat up.

He pulled back for a moment, then kissed her again with a certainty that made Della want to give up control. To give in to Luke.

Luke. She could scarcely believe it was his lips moving over hers, coaxing hers to part. As she opened to him, she could taste the sharp tang of the Shiraz, but more... She could taste him, and she couldn't get enough.

She wound her fingers into his hair and held his head in place as she attempted to deepen the kiss. Luke's lips curved against hers in a smile but he didn't let her down, responding instantly, taking her mouth hungrily. He explored, he possessed. And she urged him on, needing more and more of him, forgetting everything but the sensations sizzling through her.

He pulled away again and this time lifted his head. 'God, I almost forgot where we were.'

'Mmm.' She sighed into his shoulder.

His eyes glittered. 'Shall we go back in?'

She took a deep breath. 'Absolutely. I don't want to miss dessert.'

'We won't have to stay much longer.'

She saw the message in his eyes and didn't flinch from it.

The auction had finished when they re-entered. Desserts were being distributed, and Della darted a glance at Luke. 'Just in time.'

'The auction went well,' Tanya said as they sat. 'The signed cricket bat fetched a tidy sum. So did the football. Luke, the official photographer has arrived, and I'd like him to get a picture of you with the highest bidders for the big ticket items. Is that okay?'

'Sure. Anything you want, Tanya. You rule the roost as far as publicity is concerned.'

'Not for much longer.' She pulled a face at him. 'I hope you've thought about hiring someone else because I'm due in— How many days is it, Derek?'

'Seven.'

'I'm due in seven days, so by the time you take over from Christopher you'll be on your own.'

Della saw a smile tug at the corners of Luke's mouth. 'Duly noted, Tanya.'

'It will take someone good to handle the job.'

'I've set my sights on a very special someone. She'll be able to handle it. No worries.'

Della grinned, secure in the knowledge he rated her ability to do the job. Not that she would disappoint. She'd throw herself into learning the ropes. They hadn't discussed salary, but it didn't matter. As long as it covered her mortgage, she'd be happy. The future would take care of itself.

She watched Luke and Tanya leave the room, ate dessert, then settled back to listen to the band which had set up on stage. Guests took to the dance floor, and she was wondering whether Luke would want to dance when she felt a light tap on her shoulder. Twisting in her seat, she blinked up at a tall dark-haired stranger. An instant later, she recognised him—a former client and owner of an electronics business. She'd stage-managed the opening of his new premises, a small but successful media event.

Sliding her napkin from her lap, she stood to shake his hand. 'Jeremy. How nice to see you.'

'It's *very* nice to see you, Della. In fact, I've been trying to contact you.'

'You have?'

'I'll explain…if you'll dance with me.' He held out a hand as if he expected her to agree.

'All right.'

When Jeremy pulled her close, she tensed, but tried not to make her discomfort too obvious. She couldn't fault his dancing, but didn't enjoy herself one bit. It felt wrong to be this close to any man but Luke.

After some small talk, she asked, 'What did you want to explain, Jeremy?'

'I'm opening another branch and I'd like you to handle the arrangements again.'

'I see. I'm afraid I've left—'

'I know. I called your old office looking for you. It was a stroke of luck seeing you here tonight. You will do it, won't you?'

'I don't think it would be ethical of me, Jeremy. You're the firm's client, after all. Not mine.'

He raised his eyebrows. 'Now, if I want to transfer my patronage, surely it's my prerogative? It's not as if you poached me, is it?'

'I suppose not, but actually I've been offered another job and I'll be unavailable.'

His face fell. 'I'm sorry to hear it.'

By the time she made her way back to the table, Luke had returned and he looked grim. A muscle twitched in his cheek.

'What's wrong?' she asked, leaning close.

He stared at her, his grey eyes dark. 'Who was that?'

'Who—you mean Jeremy? He used to be a client.'

'He didn't hold you like a client.'

She frowned. Then the penny dropped. He was jealous! Warmth spread through her in waves. But, at the same time, it was wrong. She wanted him. Tonight. But a relationship wasn't on the cards for them. They wouldn't belong to each other. She couldn't give him what he wanted. Confusion made her stomach swish and her heart thump.

'You were doing a lot of talking,' he said.

'He offered me some work.'

His eyes narrowed. 'Did you agree to do it?'

'No, of course not. I just accepted a new job, didn't I?'

His face relaxed a little. 'Will you be seeing him again?'

She squeezed his hand where it rested on the table. 'No, I won't be seeing him again.'

He exhaled a long breath. 'Dance?'

'Thought you'd never ask.'

Now this felt right, she thought, as she relaxed into Luke's arms. The scent of him surrounded her. She absorbed it through her pores. She wanted to press closer, to feel the length of his body against hers, but she restrained herself. Barely.

After some time, she looked up. She knew her eyes would transmit what she felt, what she wanted. They had to. Just like his eyes were doing. She bit her lip as he bent his head lower.

'Are you ready to leave?' he murmured near her ear.

'I'm ready,' she whispered.

Luke led her from the dance floor. They made a brief stop at the table to say goodnight, then departed as quickly and as unobtrusively as possible.

CHAPTER TWELVE

In Luke's car, Della's excitement built in the silence between them. Talking would have spoilt the moment, destroyed the anticipation. They didn't need to discuss where they were going and what they were going to do when they got there. They both knew.

She darted a glance at Luke. Common sense had deserted her. She knew it was just one night and could never be more, but she had no doubts, would have no second thoughts. This was what she wanted, and if she didn't have this one night she would regret it for the rest of her life. Nothing mattered for the moment but the throbbing excitement racing through her. She had no thought for the future, not even for tomorrow. She cared only about the aching need inside her for this man.

When they arrived, Della reached for the car door. As on Wednesday, Luke stopped her with a touch. She met his gaze and waited.

'Just so there's no misunderstanding,' he said, his voice scratchy. 'If I come to the door with you, it won't be as a friend. I won't leave you there and walk away.'

She placed a hand against his cheek, the skin firm under her fingers. 'Don't walk away. Not tonight. I couldn't stand it.' She touched her lips to his and drew back. 'Kiss me.'

He caught her hand and slid it from his cheek to his mouth,

pressing his lips against her palm. Then he dropped her hand and kissed her lips with the gentlest movement of his mouth against hers.

A trembling started in her stomach.

'More,' she whispered against his mouth. 'I want more of you.'

With a groan, he slipped his arms around her and pulled her close. She melted into him and, when he took her mouth, his lips and tongue caressing her, desire swept through her in a burst of heat and need.

Eventually, she dragged herself away and out of the car. They made it into the house without touching again, but as soon as the front door closed he pushed her back against it and kissed her. Hard. His kiss was more possessive than she'd known a kiss could be. She was his. She belonged to him. Always had. And, tonight, she could tell he knew it too.

But after tonight...

No! She wouldn't think that far ahead. She'd just take this one night because...because she could.

He stepped back, breathing heavily, and the hunger in his gaze as it trickled over her sent awareness rippling through her body.

'I love your shoulders,' he said, stroking his hands across them from her neck to her upper arm and back again. 'They drive me crazy. Every time I see them, I...'

'Yes?' she said breathlessly, when his words trailed off.

He smiled, his eyes burning with grey fire. She hadn't known such a look existed.

He placed his lips against her shoulder and a long, shuddering sigh escaped from her. His hands slid around her back and she felt the zip of her dress slide down. As his lips moved lower, her head fell back and she knew stopping was no longer an option. Regrets could wait. Tomorrow would have to take care of itself. She was on the brink of the most wonderful experience of her life, and she was not going to let anything spoil it.

Composed, calm, cool—not tonight. Definitely not tonight. White-hot with desire, out of control and loving it.

'Let's go upstairs,' she murmured.

He carried her. She'd never been carried before. He made her feel precious. No one had ever made her feel so special. When she finally lay naked beneath him on the cool cotton duvet-cover, she felt tears sting her eyes, but she wouldn't let them fall. This was too wonderful a moment to spoil it with tears.

'I can't believe this is really happening.' Her voice shook. 'After so many years of wanting—'

He jerked back. 'What?'

She closed her eyes, knowing what she'd done.

'Don't stop,' she said, arching her back to rub her body against his. 'Please.'

He rolled off her and stretched out on his side. She felt the cool air rushing in to take the place of his hot body. Cold fear gripped her heart. Had she blown her one and only chance?

'Are you saying you wanted…this…when we were young?'

She nodded, chewing on her lip.

'I don't know what to say.' Confusion filled his eyes.

'Don't say anything.' She reached out a tentative hand and trailed it across his stomach.

He sucked in a breath. 'But if I'd known…'

'*Please,*' she said, not caring how desperate she sounded. She *was* desperate. She slid her fingers over his hip, down his thigh.

He groaned and ran his own hand across her body, catching her taut nipples and making her squirm. He resumed his former position but hesitated again. Della thought the frustration would kill her.

The next morning, Della reached for Luke but the pillow was empty. Apart from her, the bed was empty.

He'd gone.

What a fantastic, amazing, unforgettable night it had been. He'd wanted her as much as she'd wanted him. There'd been no doubt of it. His lips, his hands, his body had all told her how much he wanted her. And not just once.

She heaved an enormous sigh as she rolled towards the window. A cool breeze touched her bare skin. She lifted her head from the pillow and saw the lightweight curtains billowing inwards. The French doors stood wide open. And Luke stood in front of them. Luke, in boxer shorts and nothing else.

Mixed emotions coursed through her.

'Morning,' she said softly.

He turned and saw her. His smile was so warm she melted. He walked to the bed and she scooted over, making room for him to sit on the edge.

Bending forward, he placed a light kiss on her lips then stroked her cheek. 'Morning, sweetheart. Did you sleep well?'

She nodded. 'You?'

He grinned. 'Never so well. Della, that was the most amazing night of my life.'

She sucked in a breath before closing her eyes. 'Mine too.'

He hesitated. 'You don't look very happy about it.'

She squeezed her eyes tight. 'I am happy.'

He placed a hand on her shoulder and rubbed it in light circles. 'So, what happens next? Shall we tell everyone, or keep the news to ourselves for a while? What do you think?'

'Luke...' She swallowed hard. 'There is no news. We can't do this.'

His hand stilled. 'What?'

'We have to go back to the way we were. We have to go

back to being friends. This can't happen again. We can't have…an affair.'

She opened her eyes as she felt his weight lift from the bed. He walked to the French doors, then back again to stand looking down at her.

'What are you talking about? This wasn't a one-night stand.'

She sat up, dragging the duvet up to her shoulders. 'That's exactly what it was. We're mature adults. We know this sort of thing happens. We can get past it. We can still be friends.'

'Are you joking?' His voice rose and anger flashed in his eyes. 'You might be able to shut down your feelings like that, but I can't. If that's what you thought, you're mad.'

Maybe she was. Maybe she had been mad to think she could have her one night and still keep his friendship. She'd convinced herself it was possible. Now she wasn't so sure. But she had to try.

'Luke, be reasonable. We got a little carried away, but there's no need for that to happen again. Not now we've got it out of our systems.'

'Got it out of our systems? I can't believe I'm hearing this.' He spun away and strode to the chair in the corner where his clothes were piled.

With a shaky voice, Della tried again. 'What I'm saying is, we've been friends a long time—'

'And you told me last night that you've wanted more than friendship for most of that time.' His eyes flashed again.

She'd hoped he would forget her slip of the tongue. 'I shouldn't have said that. It was the alcohol talking.'

'You didn't drink that much. You never do.'

No. She was too scared of turning into her mother.

He dragged on his suit trousers and zipped them. 'Why didn't you stop me? It was your choice. If you didn't want this, why did you let it happen?'

'I did want it.' Her voice shook, but she cleared her throat and went on. 'I did want you. I would have thought that was obvious.'

'But only for one night?' he asked incredulously.

'That's just the way it has to be.'

He turned, fixing her with a dull grey gaze while he shoved his arms into his shirt. 'I've done it again, haven't I?'

'What?'

She stared at him, confused. He pushed his feet into shoes without taking his eyes from her.

'You're just like Yvonne. You used me for sex. That was all you cared about. You don't care about me or how I might feel about this.'

He grabbed his jacket and headed for the door.

'No!'

She heard his footsteps pound down the stairs while she scrambled out of bed and searched for her robe. Before she could slip it on, she heard the front door slam.

She sank onto the edge of the bed. She wouldn't chase after him. Perhaps it was for the best like this. If she'd caught him and explained the real reason, he might have said it didn't matter that she couldn't have children.

But it did matter.

He might wear her down. He might convince her to give them a chance. But she'd always know it mattered to him, and it would matter to her.

That was a very good reason for maintaining her silence.

She wasn't the woman for him. He needed a wife who'd give him a family. The loving, happy family he deserved, just like the one he came from.

She'd thought long and hard during the previous few days and, no matter how she'd debated it, she'd come to the same conclusion. She had to let Luke go.

All she'd wanted was one night to remember, but she'd destroyed their friendship. She'd fooled herself into believing one night was possible, and in her selfishness, her need, she'd pushed aside the thing that mattered most to her.

And, in doing so, she'd hurt Luke.

She'd seen the pain in his eyes. He'd allowed himself to trust a woman again and she'd thrown his trust back in his face. He'd never forgive her and she didn't blame him.

After sitting for what seemed like hours, she became aware of waves bursting onto the beach below. The sounds of a storm blowing in.

Zombie-like, she swung her legs to the ground, tied the towelling robe around her waist and crossed the room to swing the doors closed.

It should have been the happiest morning of her life. The morning after the man she loved had shown her all night—again and again—that he cared deeply for her. Instead, she had a constriction in her throat and a sickness in her stomach. Suddenly, she grew cold and her legs threatened to give way. She stumbled back to the bed, crumpled onto it and accepted the terrifying blackness of despair.

A week later, Della woke from a restless sleep to the distant sound of a phone ringing. She ignored it. She'd become an expert at ignoring phones. Reaching for the box of tissues by the bed, she grabbed a handful and blew her nose. She'd been screening calls all week, not wanting to talk to any members of the Brayford family. She didn't know where her rift with Luke left her as far as they were concerned.

As for Lyn… She hoped they'd be friends again, but for now she couldn't bring herself to talk to her.

A dry sob broke from her chest. How could she ask her friend to share the deepest, darkest sadness of her life when it involved her brother so completely?

As the mound of tissues on the floor grew, she rolled out

of bed. She knew she'd survive no matter how gutted she felt now. She'd lived through bad times before, and they'd taught her that much at least. She would bury her feelings. She would survive.

Della showered, dressed and tidied the bedroom. She'd been working quietly but diligently during the week and had finished Mary's promotional products. She'd delivered the final version of each to the printer the day before, and had earned the right to some time for herself today. She'd start by sitting outside with a book for a while. It would do her good to escape into a fictional world, and the fresh sea air would blow some cobwebs away. She went to the French doors.

As she leaned on the iron balustrade, she spotted a familiar shape standing halfway down the beach. Luke. Staring at her house.

Her blood ran cold, but at the same time her heartrate sped up. He hadn't phoned. He hadn't tried to contact her all week. What was he doing here now? And what should she do? Should she go to him?

Before she'd made up her mind, he moved, and she knew instinctively he would head for her door. Pushing off the balustrade, she took several deep, steadying breaths before going down to meet him.

He looked sick. She hated to admit it, but they looked as bad as each other. Pushing the door wide, she gestured to him to come inside.

He shook his head.

After a moment, he said, 'Do you want to go for a walk?'

She hesitated, then grabbed her keys, deliberately leaving the mobile phone behind on the hall table.

They strolled onto the sand, more than an arm's length distance between them, and walked for a couple of minutes before Luke spoke.

'I wanted to let you know that your job is safe. In case you were wondering.'

She looked down at her feet rather than see his reaction as she asked, 'Do you think it's a good idea for us to work together?'

'We won't be working together.'

'Oh?'

'I'm going back to India.'

She stopped and turned towards the ocean, folding her arms. 'You don't have to do that. I can find another job.' As difficult as it would be to give up her dream job, she should be the one to move aside.

'I'm not doing it for you.'

She dug her toes into the damp sand as she faced him. Every breath felt like sandpaper as she dragged it in. She thought her heart would break at the sight of his stony face.

He picked up a flat pebble and skimmed it across the water's surface.

'Who will take the CEO's position?'

'Phyllis and I will cover it between us until we can find a replacement.'

'And the intention is that I'll work for the replacement?'

'Yes.'

Silence settled between them, but neither moved. It wasn't the easy, peaceful silence that had characterised their friendship.

After several long moments, Della moistened her lips. She could stand the silence no longer. 'When are you leaving?'

'I'm flying to Melbourne later today to talk to Phyllis. I'll catch an international flight from there tomorrow.' He skimmed another stone.

'Luke…'

'I don't think there's anything else to say, Della.'

'Except, I'm sorry.'

He sighed. 'Yeah, me too.'

She thought she saw his eyes glisten with moisture before he turned abruptly and strode away from her. She stood in the same spot till her knees wobbled and then she sat on the sand, gazing at the horizon, but all she could see was the mess she'd made of her life.

CHAPTER THIRTEEN

LUKE dragged the shirts from their hangers and flung them into the suitcase. He'd made the necessary phone calls, set everything in motion. He'd be gone by the end of the day.

He dropped a pile of T-shirts into the case and strode to the window for one last look across the city to the hills.

It wasn't as if he'd never be back. He'd visit his parents, Lyn and her family, Megan and Poppy. But not Della. Never again.

Pain tore through him. His chest ached like it would cave in. Leaving Yvonne hadn't hurt this bad. He pressed his palms against the cool glass. He'd finally worked out why he'd always felt so good around Della. It had taken him long enough, but he'd eventually understood that the physical attraction he'd fought against was only the tip of the iceberg.

But what good had it done him?

One spectacular night of love-making and then…nothing. Everything they'd had, they'd destroyed with that one night.

And still he didn't understand. Why had she slept with him and then thrust him away, refusing even to consider a relationship?

A memory surfaced. The day they'd brought the children back to this room to sleep, she'd stood in front of this window and told him she'd been in love. Had she lied when she'd said it was over? Was there someone else? And, if so, what reason could she have for concealing the fact from him?

Conflicting emotions chased each other through his consciousness. He couldn't decide whether her loving someone else made the rejection hurt more or less. He just knew it hurt like hell.

He pushed against the glass and straightened away from it. He had packing to finish, family to see, a plane to catch.

Later, he parked the Saab outside Lyn's house and walked to the door with a heavy heart. He knew Lynnie would be upset and this was the easy part; he still had to break the news to his mother.

'But I don't understand,' Lyn said once he'd explained his change of plan. 'I thought you were here to stay. What's changed in the last week?'

He sighed. 'A lot.'

'What? What?'

To his horror, he saw tears in his sister's eyes. Frowning, he said, 'I wasn't going to say anything, but...'

'But?'

He took Cassie from her and sat on the sofa, bouncing the baby on his knees. 'Have you spoken to Della this week?'

'No. She hasn't returned my calls. She must be really busy with the freelance work she's doing.'

He looked up. 'I don't think that's the reason.'

'Then...?' Lyn gave him a puzzled look before her eyes widened. 'Oh my God. Have you two argued? What about? Why?'

He grimaced. 'Lynnie, I don't want to talk about it. I just thought you should know that she might need a friend right now. I think you're all she has left.'

Lyn moved to sit next to him. 'Luke, what have you done?'

With a deep sigh, he said, 'It has to be me, does it?'

'Yes.'

'Thanks for the confidence.' He tried to make light of it, but he felt anger spurt up from deep inside and though he hadn't meant to reveal his feelings, he blurted, 'All I did was fall in love with her.'

Lyn squealed, startling Cassie. She took her daughter from his hands and rocked her on her shoulder. 'Then what did you do?'

'Nothing.' He shrugged. 'Where's Jamie?'

'With his father. Don't change the subject. This is my best friend you're talking about. I want to know what you've done to upset her.'

He closed his eyes and leaned back, weary suddenly. 'I did nothing. I've thought about this all week, and I can only assume she's still in love with that other man.'

'What other man?' Lyn gaped at him.

'I don't know. Someone she loves but can't have. She wouldn't say who.'

'This is news to me,' Lyn said. 'I don't believe it. Surely I would have known?'

'Maybe not.' He opened his eyes slowly. 'I think Della's better at hiding things than anyone I've ever known.'

'You say you love her... Do you want to marry her?'

He turned to face Lyn. 'I wanted to. I wanted her to be the mother of my children.'

'But Dell can't—'

Lyn stopped. Her words hung in the air. Her eyes wouldn't meet his.

'She can't what?'

'I promised.'

His mind raced. His eyes narrowed. 'Can't have children?'

Lyn's pained expression told him the truth.

Why hadn't Della told him? He thought back to their conversation in the park. He'd known it was all a sham when she'd said she didn't like children. She'd been hiding the fact she couldn't have them.

Pieces of the puzzle fell into place. He'd told her about the disagreement with Yvonne, but he hadn't told her the full extent of it. But if she'd known...would it have made a difference?

'Do you think Della would have pushed me away rather than tell me this?'

Lyn shrugged. 'She doesn't want anyone to know. She feels like a failure as a woman.'

His stomach churning, he stood up. 'I have to go.'

'Where? To see Dell?'

He nodded.

'Don't tell her I leaked her secret. She'll hate me.'

'I won't.'

'And don't upset her any more than you have already.'

He wrapped his sister and niece in a hug. 'Thank you, Lynnie.'

For the second time that day, Luke parked near Della's house and walked along the esplanade. Earlier his steps had been slow and heavy. This time he hurried past the parked cars and covered the last few metres at a run. He knew it was a long shot, but if he left without finding out he'd always wonder. And instinct told him he had to do this.

Della didn't answer the door.

He pushed his hand through his hair impatiently. Had she gone out, or was she avoiding him? He spun around, scanning the beach as he tried to decide his next move.

And then he saw her.

Della was still in the same spot he'd left her earlier. The tide was on its way in, and the water's edge had come very close to her feet. But she hadn't moved.

Not wanting to startle her, he waited till he was a short

distance from her and called her name softly. Her head came up but she didn't look round. He wondered if she thought she was dreaming. He stopped at her shoulder and spoke her name again.

She turned to gaze up at him and he saw her tear-ravaged face. His heart squeezed, and he hoped…he just hoped his guess was right.

'You're going to get wet.'

'What?'

'The tide.'

He gestured at the water. She looked around, then jumped to her feet and stepped back.

Then she turned slowly. 'What are you doing here? Shouldn't you be on a plane?'

'Do you want me to go?'

'I…' Her face contorted.

He waited for a moment. When she seemed unable to speak, he said, 'Can I tell you something?'

She shrugged.

'Can I tell you why Yvonne and I broke up?'

He saw her swallow deeply. 'You did already.'

'Not the whole story.' He glanced along the beach. In one direction a man throwing a ball into the waves for a dog, and in the other a young couple huddled together near the rocks, were the only people visible.

'At the orphanage where I was based—the one you saw in my film—there are some great kids, but I can't deny that one of them, Sharma, has always been my favourite. She's about the same age as Jamie and she's so sweet.'

'You mentioned her before. You said she was your shadow.'

He nodded. 'I've known her since she was a baby. I was only visiting back then, but I happened to be there when she was brought in. She'd been abandoned by her parents, and…' He lifted his palms. 'What can I say? I was a pushover.'

She stared back at him.

'When Yvonne and I married, I saw it as an opportunity to give Sharma a real home. A loving, caring one.' He sighed. 'Something she'd never known.'

Understanding lit her eyes. 'You wanted to adopt her?'

'I can't tell you how much I wanted to. But I made the mistake of assuming Yvonne would feel the same way.' Pain at the memory made him pause. 'And she didn't.'

She frowned. 'So you had to give up the idea?' She lifted a hand, but he saw her hesitate, then drop it to her side.

'Yes. A single man can't adopt a little girl.'

'No, of course not.'

'I applied for the CEO's position before Yvonne and I broke up. My intention was that we'd bring Sharma back here to Adelaide and give her the best of everything.'

She nodded. 'And that's why you split up?'

'It was a large part of the reason. As I said before, we discovered we had very different opinions on some fundamental issues, and this was one of them.'

'I see. But why are you telling me this? Why now?'

He made an impatient movement. 'I don't know. I thought...something told me you'd understand.'

She lifted her dark eyes and searched his face for a moment. 'I understand that you didn't get what you wanted. I'm sorry for that, Luke. Unfortunately, it happens to all of us,' she said softly, her voice little more than a whisper

With his chest tightening and his heart beating fast, he stepped closer and reached for her hand. She didn't pull it away, and hope sprang to life in his belly.

'Della, what do *you* want?'

She shook her head. 'I don't think that's relevant.'

'It is. To me, it's very relevant.'

She shook her head again and he sighed.

'Answer me this, then—how do you feel about adoption?'

'I…' She grimaced. 'I haven't given it any thought.'

'Will you think about it? For me?'

She dropped her gaze to their joined hands, then lifted it again. He saw the stricken look on her face, and her sad eyes where tears lurked behind the lashes. 'You *know*, don't you?'

He jerked his shoulders without speaking.

'Lyn told you?'

'Not exactly. She tried not to.'

She gasped. 'How could she?'

'Listen, I don't really know anything. I've surmised that you have a problem bearing children. Is it true?'

She gave a single nod then looked away.

'Oh, sweetheart.' He rubbed his thumb tenderly across the back of her hand, and with his free hand cupped her cheek, tracing the puffiness beneath her eye. 'Did something happen to you? Is there a medical reason?' he asked gently.

She dragged in a shaky breath. 'I had ovarian cancer.'

He stiffened. His hands stopped mid-caress. 'And I didn't know about this? Why didn't anyone tell me?'

Shaking her head, she said, 'Only Lyn knew, and she kept quiet about it because I made her promise. I didn't tell your mum. I knew she'd be devastated. I didn't want her to worry.'

'Of course she would. She loves you like a daughter. But you shouldn't have gone through it alone.'

'Not alone. Lyn's support meant a lot to me.' Her voice trembled.

He tipped up her chin and looked into her eyes. 'Are you completely well now?'

She nodded. 'I'm still here. I survived. I got through it. I have to be grateful for that. And now I have to live with the fact that I can't have children.'

Tears streaked her cheeks. He'd never seen her cry, he realised. He'd seen her come close to tears, but in all the time he'd known her he'd never actually seen her cry, and it did things to his insides.

'How long have you known this?'

'It was always a possibility, but I found out for sure on the day you arrived back here.'

'Oh, Shrimp. I'm so sorry.' Pulling her close, he wrapped his arms around her. When she rested her cheek on his chest, he felt a surge of emotions so strong he thought they'd overwhelm him. He closed his eyes for a moment till his heart settled back into its normal rhythm.

Loosening his hold, he leaned back to look at her. He swallowed deeply. 'I could have lost you before I found you. I hate knowing this.'

She gave a little moan. 'I still don't understand why you're here.'

'Because I love you.'

'Luke—'

'What I had with Yvonne wasn't love... Well, you know all that. You worked it out before me.'

'Don't do this, Luke. I'm not right for you.'

'Not right for me?' He gave a brief, puzzled laugh.

'I'm...faulty goods. Flawed.'

His grip on her tightened. 'Jeez, Della. Don't say that. You're...the right side of perfect.'

'Haven't you been listening to me? I can't have children.'

'Haven't you been listening to me? If you'll marry me, and if you agree, we can adopt Sharma. And maybe more children from the orphanage. It's up to you how many.'

'You don't want children of your own?'

He shook his head.

'You really want to marry me? This isn't just a pity proposal?' Tears were still streaming down her face as if she had no control over them.

'I really want to marry you. I need you, Della. I like who

I am when I'm around you. You make me feel good about myself and, believe me, that takes some doing.'

'But you are a good man, Luke. You're the kindest, most thoughtful, most generous man I've ever met.'

He shook his head and managed a brief laugh.

'If not for you, I wouldn't be who I am today,' she said.

'Don't give me credit for your hard work. You did it all yourself.'

'But you made me believe I could do it, make a life of my own, one that was completely different from my parents' life. Without you…' She made a hopeless gesture. 'Without you, who knows what I would have become?'

'You would have become the beautiful, wonderful woman you are now.'

'You think I'm beautiful?'

He threw back his head and laughed. 'Are you kidding? I always did. In fact, I suspect I always loved you. I just didn't know it. Or maybe this love was lying dormant, waiting for the right time to come to life. I don't know,' he said, tightening his hold again so he could feel her body crushed against his. 'But I do know I fancied you like mad.'

She gasped. 'No. Did you?'

'I'm afraid so. How does it feel to know you were the object of a teenage boy's fantasies?'

'Um, wonderful.'

He laughed, then became serious again. 'And when you said you'd wanted me for years too…it shook me to the core.'

'It was true.'

'Why didn't you give me a hint? I can be pretty dumb.'

She shook her head. 'There were so many reasons. It doesn't matter now.'

'All those years I was away, I was always looking for something, and none of the women I met could give it to me.' He took a deep breath. 'After Yvonne, I thought I was better off alone, but now I know much better. You've made me see that I do need someone else to be happy.'

After a long moment of silence, Luke loosened his hold.

'Della...you haven't said you love me. Is it because of that guy?'

'What guy?'

'That's the second time you've looked at me like you don't know who I mean.'

Stepping back, he let his arms drop to his sides. 'You told me you were in love with someone. A man who didn't love you back.'

'Oh!' She gave him a strange look. 'Him.'

'Can you forget him?'

'I've only loved one man in my whole life and I have no intention of forgetting him, not ever.'

'So...' He stared down at her, his eyes glittering.

'It's you, Luke.'

He hesitated. 'There's no one else?'

'No!'

He kissed her then. A brief but deep kiss. 'Good, because you're mine, and I don't want you to forget that.'

'As if I could. I love you, Luke.'

Della felt the furious pounding of his heart, and after a moment she lifted her head from his chest. 'You really don't mind that I can't have children?'

He sighed. 'Can we agree that, if I answer this question now, it will be the last time you ever ask it?'

She gave a hesitant nod.

'Ever?' he said with narrowed eyes.

'All right. I promise.'

'I do mind. Very much. For you. I think it was important for you to have a baby because of your mother. So you could know the kind of love you never had.'

Tears slid down her cheeks unchecked. He understood

why the bad news had devastated her. And she loved him all the more for understanding. Suddenly, the sick feeling in her stomach eased and the lump in her throat disappeared.

He stroked the tears away with his finger, then smiled. 'But you have lots of love to give our adopted children, and they're going to love you right back.'

After a slight hesitation, he said, 'As for me, no. I do not care in the slightest that there won't be any little Brayfords with my genes. It's simply not important to me. It's far more important to give a good, loving home to children who really need it.'

He smiled then. 'I hope you're satisfied with my answer, because it's the last one you'll ever get to that question.

She nodded. 'I'm more than satisfied.'

He dropped to his knees in the sand, taking both her hands in his.

'Della, my darling little Shrimp, you've taught me so much over a long time. You taught me to have compassion for those less fortunate.'

Her throat tight, she clamped a hand over her mouth.

'Now you've taught me how real love feels.' He kissed her palms in turn. 'I want to teach *you* something, too.'

She waited, holding her breath.

'I want to teach you how to be loved. I want to give you the love you should have had when you were growing up. And I want to give you all of my love, for the rest of my life.'

'Oh, Luke.'

'Will you marry me?'

She dropped to her knees. Her legs wouldn't have held her any longer.

'Yes,' she said through the tears that forced their way out despite her best efforts. 'I will be honoured to marry you, Luke.'

He kissed her.

'And you do like the idea of adoption?'

She nodded. 'I do. I might have known my parents, but I do know what it's like to be abandoned.'

He kissed the top of her head.

'I want to be the best mother Sharma could have.'

'You will be.'

'Do you still want to move back to India?'

He smiled. 'Not now.'

'We can move if you want to.'

Shaking his head, he said, 'I'm home. I've found what I was looking for.'

EPILOGUE

DELLA stared through the taxi window at the traffic of Calcutta, a seething mass of humanity. Cars, rickshaws, battered buses, overflowing trams, ancient trucks, trolleys, cows, goats and people. And, as they approached an intersection, the incongruous sight of a police officer in white gloves directing the chaos.

She reached for Luke's hand. She needed the comfort of his presence on this momentous day, but she couldn't take her eyes from the scene outside—makeshift shelters of plastic sheeting and bamboo which, Luke had told her, were inhabited by whole families. So many people, some barefoot, others in suits, men in turbans or crocheted caps, women in saris, some graceful, others old and bent. In the shade and on the corners, beggars with their tins.

Young girls running through the crowd, smiling and giggling as they asked for coins. Would Sharma look like one of these girls?

It was terrifying, yet the unrelenting energy and the smiles generated a positive vibe that made her sit forward, eager to reach their destination.

She dragged her attention from the window at last and turned to smile at her husband. She could hardly believe they were married already, but neither had wanted to wait.

When Luke put his arm around her, she snuggled closer. 'I'm excited, but I'm scared as well,' she said.

Luke opened his mouth to speak, then shook his head.

'What? What were you going to say?'

He sighed. 'I was going to tell you not to be scared but, the truth is, I am too.'

'You?' She gave a brief laugh. 'You're afraid of nothing.'

He pulled her tighter against him. 'I'm terrified that you'll change your mind. That you won't want to go through with this.'

'I won't change my mind.'

'I've known Sharma all her life. It's different for you.'

She reached up to stroke his cheek. 'Don't worry.' She laughed. 'Suddenly, I'm not scared at all. I know it's going to be fine.'

The taxi lurched off the main road.

Della looked ahead, then back at Luke. 'Is this it?'

He nodded.

Rickety gates swung open and the taxi drove through slowly, coming to a standstill in a space surrounded by assorted buildings. Within seconds they were surrounded by hundreds of shouting, laughing children.

Luke quickly paid the driver before climbing out of the vehicle. Della emerged on the other side, and tiny hands grabbed at her. She stood for a moment, bemused, but as the taxi left the children deserted her and crowded Luke, shouting his name. He crouched down and disappeared under a swarm of wriggling, giggling bodies.

A moment later, he stood up again, and now he had a child in his arms. He turned to her and smiled. Della's gaze was fixed on the little girl as he crossed the space to her. She had gorgeous brown eyes, and instinct told Della it would be easy to spoil her.

Luke whispered in Sharma's ear and she gave Della a gap-toothed grin. Just like Jamie's. Della had a glimpse of the future, of Lyn and herself comparing the progress of their children while the cousins played together. She nearly choked on the lump of emotion that rose to her throat. Love for the family she'd thought she'd never have bubbled inside her, ready for release. Luke held out his free arm and she walked into a group hug with her husband and their daughter, knowing she could safely let it out.

* * * * *

**Every Life Has More
Than One Chapter**™

Award-winning author Stevi Mittman delivers another
hysterical mystery, featuring Teddi Bayer, an irre-
pressible heroine, and her to-die-for hero, Detective Drew
Scoones. After all, life on Long Island can be murder!

*Turn the page for a sneak peek
at the warm and funny fourth book,
WHOSE NUMBER IS UP, ANYWAY?,
in the Teddi Bayer series,
by STEVI MITTMAN.
On sale August 7*

CHAPTER 1

"Before redecorating a room, I always advise my clients to empty it of everything but one chair. Then I suggest they move that chair from place to place, sitting in it, until the placement feels right. Trust your instincts when deciding on furniture placement. Your room should "feel right."

—TipsFromTeddi.com

Gut feelings. You know, that gnawing in the pit of your stomach that warns you that you are about to do the absolute stupidest thing you could do? Something that will ruin life as you know it?

I've got one now, standing at the butcher counter in King Kullen, the grocery store in the same strip mall as L.I. Lanes, the bowling alley cum billiard parlor I'm in the process of redecorating for its "Grand Opening."

I realize being in the wrong supermarket probably doesn't sound exactly dire to you, but you aren't the one buying your father a brisket at a store your mother will somehow know isn't Waldbaum's.

And then, June Bayer isn't your mother.

The woman behind the counter has agreed to go into the freezer to find a brisket for me, since there aren't any in the case. There are packages of pork tenderloin, piles of spare ribs and rolls of sausage, but no briskets.

Warning Number Two, right? I should be so out of here.

But no, I'm still in the same spot when she comes back out, brisketless, her face ashen. She opens her mouth as if she is going to scream, but only a gurgle comes out.

And then she pinballs out from behind the counter, knocking bottles of Peter Luger Steak Sauce to the floor on her way, now hitting the tower of cans at the end of the prepared foods aisle and sending them sprawling, now making her way down the aisle, careening from side to side as she goes.

Finally, from a distance, I hear her shout, "He's deeeeeeaaaad! Joey's deeeeeaaaad."

My first thought is *You should always trust your gut.*

My second thought is that now, somehow, my mother will know I was in King Kullen. For weeks I will have to hear "What did you expect?" as though whenever you go to King Kullen someone turns up dead. And if the detective investigating the case turns out to be Detective Drew Scoones... well, I'll never hear the end of that from her, either.

She still suspects I murdered the guy who was found dead on my doorstep last Halloween just to get Drew back into my life.

Several people head for the butcher's freezer and I position myself to block them. If there's one thing I've learned from finding people dead—and the guy on my doorstep wasn't the first one—it's that the police get very testy when you mess with their murder scenes.

"You can't go in there until the police get here," I say, stationing myself at the end of the butcher's counter and in front of the Employees Only door, acting as if I'm some sort of authority. "You'll contaminate the evidence if it turns out to be murder."

Shouts and chaos. You'd think I'd know better than to

throw the word *murder* around. Cell phones are flipping open and tongues are wagging.

I amend my statement quickly. "Which, of course, it probably isn't. Murder, I mean. People die all the time, and it's not always in hospitals or their own beds, or…" I babble when I'm nervous, and the idea of someone dead on the other side of the freezer door makes me very nervous.

So does the idea of seeing Drew Scoones again. Drew and I have this on-again, off-again sort of thing…that I kind of turned off.

Who knew he'd take it so personally when he tried to get serious and I responded by saying we could talk about *us* tomorrow—and then caught a plane to my parents' condo in Boca the next day? In July. In the middle of a job.

For some crazy reason, he took that to mean that I was avoiding him and the subject of *us*.

That was three months ago. I haven't seen him since.

The manager, who identifies himself and points to his nameplate in case I don't believe him, says he has to go into *his cooler*. "Maybe Joey's not dead," he says. "Maybe he can be saved, and you're letting him die in there. Did you ever think of that?"

In fact, I hadn't. But I had thought that the murderer might try to go back in to make sure his tracks were covered, so I say that I will go in and check.

Which means that the manager and I couple up and go in together while everyone pushes against the doorway to peer in, erasing any chance of finding clean prints on that Employee Only door.

I expect to find carcasses of dead animals hanging from hooks, and maybe Joey hanging from one, too. I think it's going to be very creepy and I steel myself, only to find a rather benign series of shelves with large slabs of meat laid out carefully on them, along with boxes and boxes marked simply Chicken.

Nothing scary here, unless you count the body of a middle-aged man with graying hair sprawled faceup on the floor. His eyes are wide open and unblinking. His shirt is stiff. His pants are stiff. His body is stiff. And his expression, you should forgive the pun—is frozen. Bill-the-manager crosses himself and stands mute while I pronounce the guy dead in a sort of *happy now?* tone.

"We should not be in here," I say, and he nods his head emphatically and helps me push people out of the doorway just in time to hear the police sirens and see the cop cars pull up outside the big store windows.

Bobbie Lyons, my partner in Teddi Bayer Interior Designs (and also my neighbor, my best friend and my private fashion police), and Mark, our carpenter (and my dogsitter, confidant, and ego booster), rush in from next door. They beat the cops by a half step and shout out my name. People point in my direction.

After all the publicity that followed the unfortunate incident during which I shot my ex-husband, Rio Gallo, and then the subsequent murder of my first client—which I solved, I might add—it seems like the whole world, or at least all of Long Island, knows who I am.

Mark asks if I'm all right. (Did I remember to mention that the man is drop-dead-gorgeous-but-a-decade-too-young-for-me-yet-too-old-for-my-daughter-thank-god?) I don't get a chance to answer him because the police are quickly closing in on the store manager and me.

"The woman—" I begin telling the police. Then I have to pause for the manager to fill in her name, which he does: *Fran.*

I continue. "Right. Fran. Fran went into the freezer to get a brisket. A moment later she came out and screamed that Joey was dead. So I'd say she was the one who discovered the body."

"And you are…?" the cop asks me. It comes out a bit like who do I *think* I am, rather than who am I really?

"An innocent bystander," Bobbie, hair perfect, makeup just right, says, carefully placing her body between the cop and me.

"And she was just leaving," Mark adds. They each take one of my arms.

Fran comes into the inner circle surrounding the cops. In case it isn't obvious from the hairnet and bloodstained white apron with Fran embroidered on it, I explain that she was the butcher who was going for the brisket. Mark and Bobbie take that as a signal that I've done my job and they can now get me out of there. They twist around, with me in the middle, as if we're a Rockettes line, until we are facing away from the butcher counter. They've managed to propel me a few steps toward the exit when disaster—in the form of a Mazda RX7 pulling up at the loading curb—strikes.

Mark's grip on my arm tightens like a vise. "Too late," he says.

Bobbie's expletive is unprintable. "Maybe there's a back door," she suggests, but Mark is right. It's too late.

I've laid my eyes on Detective Scoones. And while my gut is trying to warn me that my heart shouldn't go there, regions farther south are melting at just the sight of him.

"Walk," Bobbie orders me.

And I try to. Really.

Walk, I tell my feet. *Just put one foot in front of the other.*

I can do this because I know, in my heart of hearts, that if Drew Scoones was still interested in me, he'd have gotten in touch with me after I returned from Boca. And he didn't.

Since he's a detective, Drew doesn't have to wear one of those dark blue Nassau County Police uniforms. Instead, he's got on jeans, a tight-fitting T-shirt and a tweedy sports jacket. If you think that sounds good, you should see him. Chiseled features, cleft chin, brown hair that's naturally a little sandy in the front, a smile that…well, that doesn't matter. He isn't smiling now.

He walks up to me, tucks his sunglasses into his breast pocket and looks me over from head to toe.

"Well, if it isn't Miss Cut and Run," he says. "Aren't you supposed to be somewhere in Florida or something?" He looks at Mark accusingly, as if he was covering for me when he told Drew I was gone.

"Detective Scoones?" one of the uniforms says. "The stiff's in the cooler and the woman who found him is over there." He jerks his head in Fran's direction.

Drew continues to stare at me.

You know how when you were young, your mother always told you to wear clean underwear in case you were in an accident? And how, a little farther on, she told you not to go out in hair rollers because you never knew who you might see—or who might see you? And how now your best friend says she wouldn't be caught dead without makeup and suggests you shouldn't either?

Okay, today, *finally,* in my overalls and Converse sneakers, I get it.

I brush my hair out of my eyes. "Well, I'm back," I say. As if he hasn't known my exact whereabouts. The man is a detective, for heaven's sake. "Been back awhile."

Bobbie has watched the exchange and apparently decided she's given Drew all the time he deserves. "And we've got work to do, so…" she says, grabbing my arm and giving Drew a little two-fingered wave goodbye.

As I back up a foot or two, the store manager sees his chance and places himself in front of Drew, trying to get his attention. Maybe what makes Drew such a good detective is his ability to focus.

Only what he's focusing on is me.

"Phone broken? Carrier pigeon died?" he asks me, taking

in Fran, the manager, the meat counter and that Employees Only door, all without taking his eyes off me.

Mark tries to break the spell. "We've got work to do there, you've got work to do here, Scoones," Mark says to him, gesturing toward next door. "So it's back to the alley for us."

Drew's lip twitches. "You working the alley now?" he says.

"If you'd like to follow me," Bill-the-manager, clearly exasperated, says to Drew—who doesn't respond. It's as if waiting for my answer is all he has to do.

So, fine. "You knew I was back," I say.

The man has known my whereabouts every hour of the day for as long as I've known him. And my mother's not the only one who won't buy that he "just happened" to answer this particular call. In fact, I'm willing to bet my children's lunch money that he's taken every call within ten miles of my home since the day I got back.

And now he's gotten lucky.

"*You* could have called *me*," I say.

"You're the one who said *tomorrow* for our talk and then flew the coop, chickie," he says. "I figured the ball was in your court."

"Detective?" the uniform says. "There's something you ought to see in here."

Drew gives me a look that amounts to *in or out?*

He could be talking about the investigation, or about our relationship.

Bobbie tries to steer me away. Mark's fists are balled. Drew waits me out, knowing I won't be able to resist what might be a murder investigation.

Finally he turns and heads for the cooler.

And, like a puppy dog, I follow.

Bobbie grabs the back of my shirt and pulls me to a halt.

"I'm just going to show him something," I say, yanking away.

"Yeah," Bobbie says, pointedly looking at the buttons on my blouse. The two at breast level have popped. "That's what I'm afraid of."

ATHENA FORCE

Heart-pounding romance and thrilling adventure.

A ruthless enemy rises against the women of Athena Academy. In a global chess game of vengeance, kidnapping and murder, every move exposes potential enemies—and lovers. This time the women must stand together... before their world is ripped apart.

THIS NEW 12-BOOK SERIES BEGINS WITH A BANG IN AUGUST 2007 WITH

TRUST
by Rachel Caine

Look for a new Athena Force adventure each month wherever books are sold.

HARLEQUIN®

Super Romance®

*Looking for a romantic, emotional
and unforgettable escape?*

*You'll find it this month and every month
with a Harlequin Superromance!*

Rory Gorenzi has a sense of humor and a sense of
honor. She also happens to be good with children.

Seamus Lee, widower and father of four, needs
someone with exactly those traits.

They meet at the Colorado mountain school owned
by Rory's father, where she teaches skiing and
avalanche safety. But Seamus—and his children—
learn more from her than that....

Look for

GOOD WITH CHILDREN

by Margot Early,

*available August 2007, and these other
fantastic titles from Harlequin Superromance.*

REASONS FOR REVENGE

A brand-new provocative miniseries by *USA TODAY* bestselling author **Maureen Child** begins with

SCORNED BY THE BOSS

Jefferson Lyon is a man used to having his own way. He runs his shipping empire from California, and his admin Caitlyn Monroe runs the rest of his world. When Caitlin decides she's had enough and needs new scenery, Jefferson devises a plan to get her back. Jefferson *never* loses, but little does he know that he's in a competition....

Don't miss any of the other titles from the REASONS FOR REVENGE trilogy by *USA TODAY* bestselling author **Maureen Child**.

SCORNED BY THE BOSS #1816
Available August 2007

SEDUCED BY THE RICH MAN #1820
Available September 2007

CAPTURED BY THE BILLIONAIRE #1826
Available October 2007

Only from Silhouette Desire!

HARLEQUIN®

American ROMANCE®

TEXAS LEGACIES: THE CARRIGANS

Get to the Heart of a Texas Family

WITH

THE RANCHER NEXT DOOR
by
Cathy Gillen Thacker

She'll Run The Ranch—And Her Life—Her Way!

On her alpaca ranch in Texas, Rebecca encounters
constant interference from Trevor McCabe, the
bossy rancher next door. Rebecca becomes very
friendly with Vince Owen, her other neighbor and
Trevor's archrival from college. Trevor's problem
is convincing Rebecca that he is on her side, and
aware of Vince's ulterior motives. But Trevor has
fallen for her in the process....

On sale July 2007

REQUEST YOUR FREE BOOKS!
2 FREE NOVELS PLUS 2
FREE GIFTS!

HARLEQUIN ROMANCE®

From the Heart, For the Heart

YES! Please send me 2 FREE Harlequin Romance® novels and my 2 FREE gifts. After receiving them, if I don't wish to receive any more books, I can return the shipping statement marked "cancel." If I don't cancel, I will receive 4 brand-new novels every month and be billed just $3.57 per book in the U.S., or $4.05 per book in Canada, plus 25¢ shipping and handling per book and applicable taxes, if any*. That's a savings of over 15% off the cover price! I understand that accepting the 2 free books and gifts places me under no obligation to buy anything. I can always return a shipment and cancel at any time. Even if I never buy another book from Harlequin, the two free books and gifts are mine to keep forever.

114 HDN EEV7 314 HDN EEWK

Name	(PLEASE PRINT)	
Address		Apt.
City	State/Prov.	Zip/Postal Code

Signature (if under 18, a parent or guardian must sign)

Mail to the Harlequin Reader Service®:
IN U.S.A.: P.O. Box 1867, Buffalo, NY 14240-1867
IN CANADA: P.O. Box 609, Fort Erie, Ontario L2A 5X3

Not valid to current Harlequin Romance subscribers.

Want to try two free books from another line?
Call 1-800-873-8635 or visit www.morefreebooks.com.

* Terms and prices subject to change without notice. NY residents add applicable sales tax. Canadian residents will be charged applicable provincial taxes and GST. This offer is limited to one order per household. All orders subject to approval. Credit or debit balances in a customer's account(s) may be offset by any other outstanding balance owed by or to the customer. Please allow 4 to 6 weeks for delivery.

Your Privacy: Harlequin is committed to protecting your privacy. Our Privacy Policy is available online at www.eHarlequin.com or upon request from the Reader Service. From time to time we make our lists of customers available to reputable firms who may have a product or service of interest to you. If you would prefer we not share your name and address, please check here. ☐

HR07

Coming Next Month

#3967 MARRYING HER BILLIONAIRE BOSS Myrna Mackenzie
Black sheep Carson Banick needs a wife to save his family's fortune.
Beth Crayton, Carson's feisty PA, is determined to succeed on her own,
without a man. As the attraction between them grows, Carson must decide
what's more important: saving his family, or claiming Beth's heart?

#3968 THE ITALIAN'S WIFE BY SUNSET Lucy Gordon
The Rinucci Brothers
Sensible Della Hadley should have known better than to embark on an affair
with irresistible playboy Carlo Rinucci. She knows such passion cannot last,
despite Carlo's protests that their love is forever. Can Carlo make Della his
bride before the sun sets on their affair?

#3969 HIS MIRACLE BRIDE Marion Lennox
Castle at Dolphin Bay
Shanni Jefferson doesn't do family! But when she finds herself a live-in
nanny to five little children—and working side by side with their gorgeous
guardian Pierce MacLaughlin—she begins to wonder whether family life with
this adorable brood might suit her after all.

#3970 REUNITED: MARRIAGE IN A MILLION Liz Fielding
Secrets We Keep
Popular TV presenter Belle is married to gorgeous billionaire Ivo, and lives in
a beautiful mansion. Yet beneath the veneer of her perfect life is the truth of
their marriage of convenience. But Belle is deeply in love with Ivo, and only
wishes for a baby to make their family whole.

#3971 BABY TWINS: PARENTS NEEDED Teresa Carpenter
Baby on Board
Rachel Adams's independent life is turned upside down when she's named
guardian to two orphaned twins! Then gorgeous co-guardian Ford Sullivan
turns up. Being this close to Ford makes Rachel wonder whether stand-in
mom and dad could become forever bride and groom?

#3972 BREAK UP TO MAKE UP Fiona Harper
Nick and Adele Hughes's marriage is over. But, stranded in a picturesque
cottage, they find they cannot resist the spark that has always fizzed
between them. As the twinkling firelight works its magic, Nick and Adele
discover that the wonderful thing about breaking up is making up.

HRCNM0707